FROM
THE HORSE'S
MOUTH

A Novel

Eugene Davis

Rhoman Books
Nashville, Tennessee

From The Horse's Mouth
©2002 by Eugene Davis

Published by Rhoman Books
1708 21st Ave. S. #146
Nashville, TN 37212
www.rhomanbooks.com
ISBN: 0-9721438-0-7

Printed in the United States of America

"The greatness of a nation and its moral progress can be judged by the way its animals are treated.'

Mahatma Gandhi

THIS BOOK IS DEDICATED IN LOVING MEMORY
TO MY MOTHER

A special thanks to my father for being such an honorable human being. To Judy, Anita, Aaron, and Teresa, I couldn't have done this without you. I would also like to mention some of the horses who helped inspire this book and who have gone on to greener pastures; Chief Blu Boy, Sundust's Lacey, A Touch of Class, Delight's Superstar, Special Sonata, Merry Doughboy, and so many, many others.

FROM THE HORSE'S MOUTH

ONE

JUNIOR

February's early morning chill filled the barn and steam billowed from the horse's heaving body and flared nostrils. Two men on the ground and one on his back conspired to make this young horse ready to show.

The whip cracked and the spurs dug, until welts rose on his legs and blood oozed from his side. Still, the young bay stallion refused to move. Fear leaped from his eyes, from his breath, from his sweat. The fear of the whip and spurs was overwhelmed by the fear of the excruciating pain in his front legs and feet. A greenish, greasy substance covered both fore legs from his ankles down to the coronet band and dripped in uneven streaks down his hooves. His natural hoof had been cut short and set on stacks of leather and plastic pads at an unnatural angle. The oversized pads sat on a pair of oversized and overly heavy steel horseshoes. Three pairs of stainless steel chains were wrapped around his greased up pasterns like bracelets stacked on top of one another. The chains weighed from ten to twenty ounces each and were buckled just loose enough to rub up and down when he lifted his feet. His legs burning with pain, the colt stood trembling, yet defiant.

The young horse was big for his age, strong and big boned. His father had been a World Grand Champion. Eventually, the whips and spurs had the desired effect and lathered with sweat, the frightened bay colt took a few steps. He seemed to reach for the sky with his front hooves and flip them out in front of him as if trying to throw off the chains that clung so painfully. As soon as one front hoof hit the ground, the other one was launched in the same high arc, as if the very dirt of the barn aisle was a bed of hot coals. While his front feet alternately pawed the air, his body weight shifted to the back, causing his hind feet to knuckle over from the added weight. His hocks were almost touching the ground, but with each step came a dig of the spurs and somehow, he kept going.

At the end of the barn he was slowed and jerked around for the return trip. The twisted wire 'gag' bit pulled high in his mouth, forcing his head even higher, as if he was proud of what he was doing. But it wasn't pride that filled his eyes; it was fear and pain. The horse's head and neck moved up and down unnaturally in conjunction with the pain of each step. His ears flicked forward in search of the long whip held by one of the men on the ground. As he passed these men in the middle of the barn, he could hear them encouraging the man on his back:

"That's it Sammy. Now you got him!"
"He's strokin' now."
"Look at that..."

Lying in his stall the next day the colt was thirsty, yet he did not stand to drink. His pain was greater than his thirst. He wasn't about to put any weight on his feet, not yet anyway. Maybe they would let him rest today.

In the next stall over was an old black gelding with the gray hairs of age showing prominently around his eyes and nose. He could hear the old-timer stirring, as if from a nap. Then, after stretching a bit and yawning, the old guy sipped some water from the automatic bucket and wandered over to the stall partition that separated the two horses. The upper part of the partition was a thick wire mesh, and they'd had many a good talk through that wire.

The old horse let some water dribble from between his lips as he looked down on his young friend.

"How you feelin' today Son? 'Course I think I know the answer to that. I saw what they did to you yesterday, and I heard you moanin' and groanin' most the night. You just lay there and rest, and stay off them feets as much as you can. Maybe you'd like me to tell you a story."

"That old guy sure does ramble on sometimes," thought the young bay. But he'd come to appreciate the older horse's company, and the stories he told helped keep the young horse's mind off the pain. So, he said:

"Tell me about some of your ancestors back in the olden days, back before Walking Horses were put through this torture, if there ever was such a time."

"Oh, you betcha there was such a time. And, those ain't just my ancestors, Junior, they're yours too. In fact, I can tell of a time before there ever was a Tennessee Walking Horse, back when a lot of breeds were just coming together. You know, a lot of the modern breeds have common ancestors with us.

"'Course we got a lot of the Thoroughbred in us, as do many others. We share some of the same foundation stock as the American Saddlebred and the Standardbred. Why, some of us even go back to ol' Justin Morgan hisself. Canadian Pacers, Narraganset Pacers, all these horses contributed to the blood you've got running through your veins."

As Junior listened to the old guy talk, he tried to concentrate through the pain on what he was hearing. Once in a while, he'd slip into memories of when he was running by his mama's side, not a care in the world. Just last summer, he'd been out in a big field with eight other yearlings, running and playing, eating and sleeping. That seemed so long ago now, like another lifetime.

"As I was saying," Old Timer went on, "it was right around here in what they call Middle Tennessee that the coming together of our breed really got going.

"Seems like people have always loved to show off their horses. Even back before the war between the Gray and the Blue, this area and up in Kentucky was full of good runnin' horses, and some good trotters and pacers, too! 'Course, there was always some that seemed to stand out from the rest. And you know how people are, Junior, well they just can't wait to find out who's got the fastest or prettiest, or the 'best' horses.

"If you're wonderin' how I know all these things, it's 'cause my ol' mama, she was something of an expert on stories been handed down. All the other mares and foals used to gather around her and just listen. That is, when she wasn't being real protective of me, you know, like when I was real little.

"Anyways, if it was a lazy, muggy summer afternoon, she'd be telling stories. If we were in the shed hiding from a cold winter rain, she'd be telling stories. So, before the men took me away from her, I guess I was kinda hooked, on stories I mean. From then on, whenever I ran into a new horse, especially the older ones, I'd ask them what they knew about the olden times, about our history.

"Are you with me, Junior? I guess I got away from my story a little bit. Oh well, where was I?"

"You were talking about the horses that were our ancestors, that some of them were running around here before the war between the Gray and the Blue," Junior moaned.

"Oh yeah. 'Course that war had a huge effect on us horses all by itself, a huge effect. Many good horses died in that war, killed by men and their war machines. But that's another story, Junior, another story all together.

"Besides a lot of horses dying in the war, many of them were 'taken prisoner' or stolen from both sides. This brought us some new bloodlines and sent some of our good blood up north.

"Way before the war was a horse called Tom Hal. Ol' Tom Hal, now. There'd be other Tom Hals later, descendants of his, but I'm talking about the old guy right now. He was a blue roan foaled in 1802. They say he lived forty-one years, Junior. Well, in that time he sired many great horses, both saddle horses and pacers.

"Tom Hal came from Canada to Philadelphia, Pennsylvania where a doctor from Lexington, Kentucky saw him and bought him on the spot. He rode Ol' Tom Hal home all the way from Philadelphia to Lexington. Ol' Tom Hal was such a good ridin' horse that once, to prove a point, that doctor rode him a pacin' from Lexington to Louisville in just one day, Junior, from sun to sun. The doctor won a hundred dollars for Ol' Tom Hal's efforts. And you can be sure ol' Tom got a mighty generous feeding when they got home. One day the men laid out ten rails on the ground, you know, side-by-side and kinda spaced out. Tom Hal paced over them rails and didn't touch a one. Got so's he could do it every time. Could probably do it with his eyes closed.

"Ol' Tom Hal's greatest offspring, and he had a lot of 'em, Junior, was Bald Stockings. Bald Stockings was born when the old guy was thirty-five years old, in 1837. His mama was a daughter of Isaac Johnson's Copperbottom, and out of a Thoroughbred mare.

"Bald Stockings was named for his color, Junior, like a lot of us. He was a bald-faced roan with four white socks, high headed and fast in his gaits. The reason ol' Bald Stockings is so important is that word's been handed down he was probably the very first horse to do what people would call a 'running walk'. He sired some great horses too, including the great mare Queen. Queen was the mama of such horses as Diamond Denmark, Jewel of Denmark, and King William hisself. You know, you can trace many a good saddle horse back to that group, both American Saddlebred and Tennessee Walking Horses.

"Why, even Merry Legs, about the greatest dam ever of Tennessee Walking Horses, traces back twice to Queen. So does old Roan Allen.

"By the time the war came along, there was more than a few horses doing what you might call a runnin' walk, a four-beat gait much sought after by men traveling over a long distance. A lot of these horses would pace too, of course. But it was the smoother running walk that was the better ride.

"As you know, Junior, a pace is what they call it when a horse moves his two lateral legs in unison and a trot is when the two diagonal hooves hit the ground at the same time. Now, both of these gaits, though opposite combinations, are two-beat gaits and can be quite jarring to horse and rider. You have to put a lot more spring in your step when you're landing on two feet at the same time. A four-beat gait, when each hoof is planted at a different time, is much smoother to both horse and rider 'cause the weight's more evenly distributed. Any horse can do a four-beat gait just by walking slow and relaxed. It comes natural to all of us. Of course, running or galloping is also a four-beat gait. Some horses like you and me, Junior, can walk real fast. We might lean towards one or the other, but, somewhere between that pace and trot is your four-beat runnin' walk and a smoother ride.

"There's other breeds besides us who can do a four-beat gait movin' on. First one that comes to mind is the American Saddlebred, which is about like our second cousin as far as breeds go, I guess. A lot of them can do a real smooth 'rack' and a 'slow gait' which is similar to what we do with a little less overstride behind and more hock action. They don't keep their back end on the ground as much as we do and they don't nod their heads much. Saddlebreds can usually trot real good in addition to doin' these other gaits. That also makes them different from us. There's the Missouri Foxtrotters. They do a real smooth four-beat gait called a foxtrot, of course. There's the Rocky Mountain Horses. Then, there's the foreign horses like the Peruvian Pasos and the Paso Finos. They can be real smooth and fun to watch. What they call Spotted Saddle Horses now are mostly Tennessee Walking Horses with that pretty paint color on 'em.

"Now, when I'm talkin' about our runnin' walk, Junior, I ain't talking about this so-called 'big lick' these men are trying to get you to do. No sirree. I'm talking about what comes natural, you know. You and I both got it in us, inherited it from these ol' horses I been tellin' you about. That natural runnin' walk like you did when you was a baby, like I can still do when I've a mind to with these little flat shoes on. 'Course, everybody does it a little bit different, just like men and women all walk a little different. And it probably wasn't really fully developed back then, but they were startin' to breed for it. Why, a horse with a good natural runnin' walk, or something close to it, could carry a man around on his back for miles and miles and that man wouldn't get all wore out bein' bounced around by some rough ol' trottin' or pacin' horse.

"Junior, are you with me? I know I ramble on a bit, but I always find this stuff real interestin', don't you?"

Junior had started to doze off. There was something very soothing about the old horse's rambling. He found himself kind of listening and dreaming at the same time. He seemed to be reminded of some long forgotten memory. Something he remembered, and yet couldn't quite get a hold of, like it was someone else's memory and not his. Whatever it was, this feeling he sometimes got listening to Old Timer seemed to connect him somehow to something good. It took him away, momentarily, from the hell he was living right now.

Suddenly, the stall door slid open and Jeremy stood there glaring at him, swinging a leather and chain lead shank like a pendulum from his right hand. Jeremy was an angry young man. Junior figured he'd been born that way. It was Jeremy's job to put the awful smelling chemicals on Junior's legs, along with the plastic wrap and bandages that sweated those chemicals into his flesh. Right now, he was there to gather Junior up and get him ready for Sammy to ride again.

'Why won't they let me rest today? Please don't make me get up,' Junior thought to himself.

"Okay, Junior, time to get to work. No more laying around, you done enough of that today."

Junior still lay there watching the swinging lead shank from the corner of his eye.

"Come on, git up, you lazy son of a bitch!"

He saw it coming, but it still stung. The leather end of the lead shank caught him across the shoulder. He knew the metal snap-end would come next, so he struggled to his feet, putting more weight than he meant to on his right front, sending bolts of pain up his leg. He got his bearings and steadied himself, standing on all fours with his hind legs well underneath him to take as much weight as he could off his front feet.

Jeremy snapped the lead to Junior's halter and began to lead him out of the stall. Junior moved with the painful slowness of an old horse. He would soon be two-years old. The first step nearly brought him to his knees and he pulled back on the lead while gathering his hind legs up under himself again to bear his weight. Jeremy called to William to come help out.

"And bring a whip!"

Standing in the crossties in the breezeway of the barn, Junior was the center of attention, though there were other horses being attended to. William began unwrapping the colt's bandages while Jeremy made sure he stood still. He had put the chain end of the lead shank under Junior's lip and pulled it taut. If Junior flinched, or even hinted at moving or striking out, the reaction was immediate and the chain bit into his gums. There was the hint of a smile in Jeremy's eyes as he enjoyed this power over the strong, young colt.

William undid the outer wraps, then the cotton under wraps, followed by the plastic wrap that clung to Junior's damp legs. The effect of the non-porous plastic wrap was to "sweat" the chemicals into his skin.

Junior didn't know the names of the various chemicals used to "fix" him, but he sure did know their smell and the pain that followed. Crotonal, kerosene, diesel fuel, Koppertox, DMSO and oil of mustard are some of the ingredients used these days. Koppertox is a copper-based liquid used for the treatment of thrush, a fungus that attacks horses hooves. Mustard oil has been misused since the middle 1950's when, using it for medicinal purposes, a certain Walking Horse trainer discovered it made a horse accentuate his natural walking gait. The horse picked his front feet up higher and reached more with both his front and hind legs, giving the trainer an edge in competition. This process became known in the industry as 'soring', or 'fixing' a horse. It was all down hill from there.

In 1957, the Tennessee State Legislature passed a bill outlawing the practice of soring horses to accentuate their gait. In 1960, the Walking Horse Celebration, the breed's championship show, began inspecting the horses shown for evidence of soring.

Almost fifty years after it began, the practice of soring these animals for competition is more widespread and more sophisticated than ever. In fact, as Old Timer explained to Junior, it is impossible to successfully compete in today's shows without using illegal, very painful methods of "training". The desired gait of the show Tennessee Walking Horse has evolved into an extremely artificial, man-made gait that is miles away from the beautiful, smooth, fast walk of a good, natural, un-sored horse. The show-walk of the modern performance horse, or the "big-lick" as it is called, is simply unattainable without putting the horse through a lot of pain. Junior was learning first-hand what thousands of horses across the country are put through in preparation for competition.

William threw the used plastic wrap in a barrel and started rolling up the outer bandages, while Jeremy let up on the lead shank. He let the chain slip from under Junior's lip to under his chin and let the shank hang there, ready for a disciplinary jerk.

The fresh air felt good to Junior's legs. His skin could breath again. While he enjoyed this brief respite, Jeremy removed the leather tail set. Junior's tail had been "cut", two small incisions near the base of the muscle, when he first began training, to relax his tail for showing. He was then fitted with the tail-set, which consisted of the crupper that sat up under his tail, lifting it and holding it out away from his body, and the harness that held the crupper in place. At first it had been uncomfortable, but Junior was getting more used to the tail set every day. Since he wore it practically twenty-four hours a day, he almost felt naked without it.

Jeremy hung Junior's tail set on a hook on the wall and William took his blanket off, hanging it with the tail set. Then, they both began grooming him, first the currycomb then the brush. Jeremy picked some shavings out of Junior's long black tail, then he wrapped the base of it with a red leg bandage and tied it up so it looked something like a red question mark coming out of Junior's backside. Of course, he did this tightly and none too tenderly. It seemed like everything Jeremy did had an edge of roughness, even cruelty, to it.

Junior sometimes enjoyed the feel of the rubber currycomb when William used it, especially down low behind his shoulder and that certain spot on his back. William always used a soft brush to brush him, not the stiffest one that Jeremy used.

After brushing his mane and forelock, William smoothed Junior's coat with a towel and placed a light saddle blanket on his back. Next came the saddle, a black English cutback. Junior used to shy away from these things but now he stood perfectly still. He stood with his hind feet up under him, unnaturally close to his front. Most of the show horses stood this way, Junior had noticed, in an attempt to take some weight off their abused front feet and legs.

After William put the saddle on, Jeremy painted a pre-mixed solution of Koppertox and oil of mustard onto the colt's front feet. He applied this all around the pastern area, from the ankle to the top of the hoof, with a small paint brush, careful not to get any on his hands. The Koppertox gave the mixture a bluish-green color.

Jeremy wiped his hands on a towel, then unbuckled Junior's halter and slipped on his bridle. The bit was a twisted wire, broken mouth-piece, "gag" bit. The thin wire inside his mouth was attached to two long, curved shanks on either side. When the reins are pulled back on this type of bit, the mouthpiece slides up the curve of the shank, high into the horse's mouth, causing him to raise his head. As the cold steel bit slipped into his mouth, Junior tried not to think of what was coming next.

He remembered the day he'd been brought to this barn. After a short but scary trailer ride he'd been impressed by the size of it, by the new sights and sounds and smells. He remembered wondering why all the horses were laying down.

Junior had topped the Harlinsdale sale, which made him, as a yearling, one of the hottest young prospects in the country. His new owners and trainer had very high hopes for the pretty bay colt.

Junior had desperately missed his friends at first. The young colts and fillies he'd grown up with were suddenly out of his life forever. Horses, especially show horses, don't have much control over their own lives. People rule the world and seem to be able to do whatever they want to Junior and his fellow horses. Old Timer had told him there were men and women who loved their horses and didn't abuse them. After the past few months, Junior was finding that hard to believe.

Jeremy led Junior from the clean-up area out into the barn aisle. The aisle of the barn was purposely large, so the horses could be worked inside. After tightening the girth and lowering the stirrups, it was time for the trainer to ride Junior.

Sammy Lee Belford was excited to have such a hot prospect as Junior in his barn. He felt a lot of pressure to get the most out of this colt. Expectations ran high. His owners hadn't paid such a high price for Junior for him to come in fourth or fifth at a show. They expected him to win and the show season was just around the corner.

Junior was just the type of horse they bred for these days. Big and strong, he could take a lot of abuse. He was pacey too, which is important for a show prospect nowadays. The show horse trainers don't really want a colt or filly to start out with a real natural four-beat walk anymore because by the time they sore them enough to get all the leg motion it takes to compete in today's show classes, the horse will be too 'square', reaching for a trot. After years of breeding and refining and developing a wonderful walking gait, it's the pacier, swingier, horse that is more desirable to these gimmick trainers. If he's pacey at first, he'll have more room to work with, he can handle more chemicals, and pain, and weight before he hits that trot. These artificial means will help turn his pace into a running walk.

Junior backed his ears as he saw Sammy Lee coming toward him. He could hear the man's big-roweled spurs jingle as they scraped the ground. Junior didn't like this man at all and the man knew it, but it didn't bother him. Junior was a problem to be solved, a machine to be fine-tuned, not an intelligent, feeling animal. What this man, Sammy, liked about Junior was what the bay colt could do for him. By learning how to perform his gaits in a manner that would win blue ribbons and trophies, Junior would bring the trainer acclaim for his horsemanship and training abilities. Junior's value would increase, more money would be coming in, and more horses to train. Sammy Lee Belford would stop at nothing to make this horse out-step the competition.

Junior had noticed that there seemed to be more people in the barn this morning than usual. He saw the lady with the big hat that he'd seen before. The lady and her husband were the people who had paid such a high price for Junior and brought him to Sammy for training.

Before Sammy Lee got on the colt, he said something to Jeremy about the chains. He would keep it to just one pair today, while Mrs. Armistead was there. After all, they'd hit him pretty hard yesterday, and fixed him good last night. With the stuff they had just painted on, Sammy knew one pair of chains would be enough. He was confident he'd get a lot of leg motion out of Junior today. He was right.

Sammy Lee was a heavyset man, with the smell of cheap whiskey and a too-loud laugh. When he rode, he usually wore a tractor cap with one of the horse's names on it. The trainer swung into the saddle while Jeremy held Junior's bridle and the off side stirrup. As big a colt as Junior was, he visibly sagged and almost staggered under the weight of the man. As soon as he was in the saddle, Sammy jerked on the reins and touched his spurs to Junior's sides. Almost in slow motion, Junior walked tentatively toward the end of the barn.

Sammy kept the colt in a slow "dog walk" for a few minutes. This slow walking allowed Junior's muscles to loosen up and stretch a bit before the strain of the actual workout, when they would be pushed to the limit. It also allowed him to realize how heavy and painful a little pair of six-ounce chains could feel when rubbing against very sore, hypersensitive skin.

Sammy stopped the colt and shifted in the saddle, while Jeremy adjusted the curb chain and checked the chains on the horse's feet. Junior knew the slow walking was over. Even though he knew what to expect, it was still a shock to him that his feet could hurt so much when, after saying some words to the people watching, the man dug his heels into Junior's flanks.

The first steps always seemed the worst to Junior, and once he got going he felt the spurs at every step. Sammy was really in his mouth today, keeping the colt's head up high. He jerked him around a bit until Junior settled into the rhythm the man wanted.

Junior was really reaching, with all fours. The chemicals and chains and heavy shoes were doing their job. What was so unnatural and painful to the horse was just what the people wanted to see.

The colt was crawling with his hind legs and climbing with his front. As Sammy urged him on, he got a little more speed out of Junior and also more reach. Junior's head and neck bobbed up and down in rhythm with the climbing and reaching motion of his legs and shoulders. Each painful step brought an exaggerated nod of his head, a sure sign of lameness in any other breed but a desired attribute in the show Tennessee Walking Horse.

The man's spurs never left Junior's sides, urging him on at the slightest hesitation. He kept going as the man rode him up and down the aisle several times. According to Sammy and the people watching, the colt got a little better with each pass. So far, Junior was living up to his expectations, and promised to be very competitive in his first show season.

That night back in his stall, Junior lay on his side, listening to Old Timer continue his history lesson. The old horse knew his constant chatter helped divert Junior's attention from the agony he was in. It would also do the colt good to understand something about how the Tennessee Walking Horse got to this point, of having to endure such inhumane treatment at the hands of humanity, in the name of competition. It hadn't always been this way.

Old Timer told him some more about some of the early horses that were the foundation of their breed as it developed.

"You know, Junior, I think I told you that our ancestors were a great asset to the army of the South, the men in Gray in the war between the Gray and the Blue. Well, one of the great sires of war-horses in middle Tennessee was McMeen's Traveler. He was born in 1849, and when he was five years old, his owner sold him at auction for fifteen hundred dollars. Now, that was a lot of money in those days, Junior. But let me tell you, McMeen's Traveler was a lot of horse.

"He was a strong horse, a red sorrel with one white hind sock. He could out-pace just about any horse of that time. Besides that, he was so smooth under saddle that everybody in the country wanted to breed to him.

"I heard tell that fifty-seven of Traveler's sons and daughters served in the cavalry of General Nathan Bedford Forrest. Fifty-seven, Junior. That's a lot. General Forrest was one of the most famous - and infamous - cavalry soldiers of the war, a natural born leader and a relentless thorn in the side of the Blue army. He did a lot of his fightin' right around here in Middle Tennessee. And there's no doubt in my mind that old Traveler's get had a lot to do with the general's success as a cavalry raider. No matter what they say about ol' General Forrest, the man knew horses.

"McMeen's Traveler was by ol' Stump The Dealer, who was by Timoleon, and out of a Copperbottom mare. Unfortunately, he didn't survive the war, Junior. He was kidnapped by them Blue Coats and later found dead by the side of the road. Story goes, he didn't take too kindly to bein' captured and hauled up north and it cost him his life. But most of his sons and daughters came through the war all right, and they were able to continue their inheritance and help develop our breed. In the 1860's, most all of the top racing pacers in the state could trace to Traveler.

"There are rumors that three of the greatest, and most famous, war horses of the South had some kind of Tennessee Walking Horse in 'em. At least one of them had a definite trace to us, Junior. These horses I'm talkin' about were General Robert E. Lee's Traveller, General Forrest's King Phillip, and General Stonewall Jackson's Old Sorrell.

"It's hard to picture ol' General Lee 'cept if he's sitting atop that handsome gray gelding of his. Why, the bravery and intelligence of the both of them is, of course, legendary. They were a team, Junior, just like any great horse and his rider. And, I'm sure ol' Traveller enjoyed the spotlight and the adoration the war and his talents, and those of his famous master, brought him. He was good and he knew it. Now don't get me wrong, Junior, war is a horrible and bloody business. Still, it's in times like that, that the cream rises to the top, as they say. Traveller was proud of his accomplishments and those of the General, even though they lost the war. He carried his head up high, as he should. But there was an incident after the war that brought the great horse more than an ounce of humility.

"When General Lee became President of Washington College, his Traveller was the center of attention, a little too much attention, Junior. The old horse was so famous that every student at the college wanted to get some hair from his tail to send home as a souvenir. Well they plucked the old guy's tail till there wasn't a hair left on it, embarrassin' the heck out of him. Now they say there's a price to being famous, Junior, and I guess ol' Traveller's price was having his tail plucked plum naked."

"I bet he wanted to run away and hide, alright. What about King Phillip?" Junior wondered.

"Well now, King Phillip was bought for General Forrest by the ladies of Columbus, Georgia, after he saved their homes from enemy raiders. They hand picked him for the general, and could not have found a better horse. He was a gray like Traveller, handsome and brave. He became a great fighter and an invaluable asset to General Forrest.

"After the battle of Nashville, he carried the general for five straight days without being spelled by one of the other horses, Junior. During another battle, a pistol ball caught King Phillip in the hip and he still jumped over a wrecked wagon to carry his general to safety."

"Wow, no kidding, Old Timer?" Junior asked.

"I kid you not, YoungTimer. After the war, King Phillip died of colic in Memphis where he went for a benefit show for sick and wounded soldiers. General Forrest brought the horse home, wrapped his own blanket around him, and buried him on the farm."

"He must have really loved that horse," Junior said.

"Oh, he did, Son. He surely did. And General Jackson loved his Old Sorrell, or Little Sorrell, as he was sometimes known. He was carrying General Jackson when the general was mistakenly shot by his own men at Chancellorsville. Old Sorrell, thinking the Blue men shot his master, bolted into the night toward the enemy camp. He was gone all night Junior, probably searching for the culprit. When he came back to the Gray men at dawn, he knew he would never see his famous master again.

"I don't know about you Junior, but I find it inspirin' that these great and famous war heroes could be related to us, that some of their blood could be runnin' through our veins right now. 'Course, I've known some modern day heroes in my time, too, but I'll tell you more about them sometime later on. It's a sure thing that the predecessors of the modern Tennessee Walking Horse played an important role in the war between the Gray and the Blue.

"Now, Junior, I can't begin to tell you what all those people were fightin' about back then. But I do know that war is a terrible, terrible thing and I don't ever want to be a war-horse. That particular war, however, played an important role in the formation of our breed. As I said before, many Southern horses were captured and taken prisoner by the North and visa-versa. That's how we got some of our northern blood mixed in with our southern."

Junior stood in a thicket of tall hackberry trees, a young soldier on his back. Ahead of them in a small valley was the battle. He could see the smoke, the bursts of fire from guns and cannon, the men and horses falling down, parts of them being blown away. He could hear the screams of fear, of anger, of pain. He could smell the gunpowder, the smoke, the blood, and, most of all, the death around him.

He was scared, more scared than he'd ever been in his whole life. Every nerve in his body was telling him to turn and run in the other direction. He could sense that the boy-man on his back was scared too. Still, they stood there facing the horror and ready for the charge. Off to his left, Junior could see the leader of the men on his beautiful, valiant, black mount, horse and rider as one. As the horse reared and pawed the air, the general waved his bloody sword and yelled the charge. It was at that moment that Junior caught the eye of the general's horse and realized it was Old Timer. He looked younger and stronger, but it was him, all right. As his young rider urged Junior toward the fighting, it gave him some comfort to know his old friend was there, leading the charge.

Suddenly, an explosion to his right knocked Junior to the ground. His rider was blown off his back and lay lifeless a few yards away. Junior felt a terrible pain in his lower legs and feet. It was as if they were on fire.

He struggled to move, to stand. He wanted to get away from

the fire that was burning his legs, to run to the creek and stand in the water, soothing his burning legs and feet. But, try as he may, he could not move. He couldn't stand. He couldn't run. All he could do was just lie there and let the fire consume his legs.

From a distance, he heard a voice calling:

"Junior! Junior!" What else was the voice saying? He couldn't make it out. As the voice got closer, he thought he heard: "Junior! Hey, Junior, wake up! Wake up Junior. I think you're having a bad dream."

Junior thought, 'wake up? What do you mean wake up? I'm awake all right. I'm awake and I'm laying here with my feet on fire.' Then gradually the voice got closer and through the smoke and the fog he could see Old Timer standing over him, comforting him, telling him it was over now. It was not the young, strong, fearsome Old Timer that had led the charge. This was the older, grayer, more tired version. He realized he was no longer on the battlefield, but back in his own stall.

He struggled to his feet and found that even though he was not on the battlefield, his legs still felt like they were on fire. It hurt to stand, to put weight on his front feet. Junior shook himself all over, trying to shake off the memory of the battle and the horror and pain of it all. He realized he was wet with sweat and very tired.

"Looks like that nasty ol' nightmare got a hold of you and run you all the way to hell and back, Junior. I didn't think I was ever gonna wake you up.

"Where'd she take you, anyway? You look a fright! The way you was huffin' and puffin' and snortin' and wheezin', you could have run up to Louisville, run the Kentucky Derby and run all the way home, and not look no worse for the wear than you do right now."

Junior did feel like he'd been through hell, but he knew now it had been just a bad, bad dream, a midnight run with a nightmare from out of the past. Now he had a story of his own to tell Old Timer. But he didn't feel like reliving it just yet. He would try to get some rest and tell Old Timer about his dream in the morning. Right now, he had to lie back down and get off his burning feet. He took a long drink of water and hoped that if he did fall asleep, the nightmare would not come and try to take him back to that horrible, frightening place again.

The next day when Junior told Old Timer of his experience with the nightmare, the old horse was quite impressed.

"I guess now you know what some of your ancestors lived through, Junior. Something like that could have happened right around here you know, many, many seasons ago, but still right around this area here. And, I have a sneakin' suspicion that the spirits of some of those old horses and riders is still restless enough to hook up with that nightmare of yours and try to scare the livin' daylight out of you again if you ain't careful.

"'Course you're fightin' your own battles right now, and if I'd had anything to do with that dream of yours, it would have been ol' Sammy Lee that woke up with his feet on fire. Give him a dose of his own medicine, I say. Yessir, a dose of his own medicine, see how he likes it."

TWO

SOCKS

The foaling stall was warm and magical. People from the house had been awakened early by a call from the barn. They were standing around with sleepy and shining eyes, staring at the new, dark, wet, spindly creation standing shakily on too-long, too-widespread legs.

At this point, the colt was not concerned with the people watching him. He was too busy concentrating on remaining upright as long as possible, on coordinating the movement of his four awkward legs in a motion that would take him closer to the treasure his mother was urging and nudging him toward. She was licking and cleaning him, warming him, and softly talking to him at the same time. He didn't quite understand the words she was saying, but he understood their meaning and her intent.

He lost his balance and fell hard, but the wood shavings were soft and he decided to rest where he was for a moment, with his two front legs stuck out in front of him.

"Why don't you help him, Ned?" said one of the humans.

"No, it's better if he can do it on his own. Besides, he needs to rest a bit now. He'll try again in a minute, then we'll see."

"He looks kinda brownish, think he'll be brown or black?"

"Well, I'd say black if I had to bet on it. What with his mama being black and both his granddaddies. 'Course, you never can tell, and his daddy is that pretty chestnut color, you know. They can fool you sometimes."

"I like the way those little white socks on his hind feet came out so even. And that white snip on his nose kind of gives him character, don't you think?"

"Oh, I'm bettin' he'll have plenty of character, and those socks and that snip will help him stand out from the crowd like his daddy did, especially if he can move his legs like him, too. No offense there, mama, looks like you sure done your job all right."

After he had caught his breath and a little self-confidence, the colt struggled to his feet and jerkily, haltingly moved toward breakfast. He felt his way along his mother's belly with his nose and, after a couple of false starts, reached his destination and discovered the meaning of life.

The early days were full of wonder and discovery, and were never dull. There is always something new to life, when life is so new. After the first few days in the barn, the colt and his mama were turned out with the rest of the broodmares and their offspring. They were fed hay until the pasture grass rebounded from its winter doldrums. They had a three-sided shelter to get under when the weather was bad. They had salt blocks and plenty of water. They even got a mixture of crushed oats, corn, and molasses once a day. The humans provided well for these mares and foals. These babies would grow up to be valuable show horses. Some of them would be champions.

Socks' mama was the oldest of this group of mares and had lots of stories to tell. She told stories about her days as a show horse, stories about some of her progeny and their accomplishments, and, of course, stories about the many ancestors that she was particularly proud of. Little Socks developed quite an interest in all these stories, especially the ones about his predecessors. He loved to listen to his mama and the other mares talk whenever he wasn't too busy playing, or eating, or other important stuff. Some of the other mares seemed to know a bit of history, too. Many of them expressed concern for the future of their breed. They spoke of a thing called "soring" that scared the little green apples out of little Socks.

Weaning was particularly traumatic for Socks, maybe because he was such a mama's boy. But he lived through it and continued to turn to the memory of his mama for strength. When Socks was about 18 months old, he was gelded or castrated. He was put to sleep and woke up in pain, not really understanding what had happened to him at first. While he healed quickly, his owners did not put him in training right away. He was small for his age and they waited until Socks was more than two years old to ship him to the training stables of Ellis Walsh near Franklin, Tennessee.

Shortly after his training began, Socks found out a little about this "soring" thing he had heard about. He had tried to do what the trainers wanted him to do, but apparently that wasn't enough. They wanted more action from his legs, more "walk", more "strut". Ellis's assistant, Gerald, put a few drops of oil of mustard on his pastern area. Socks felt a burning sensation that grew in intensity as he was ridden around the barn aisle. His attention was focused on that burning feeling on his feet, and he began to lift his front legs higher and stride more with his hind. The difference in movement, though not drastic at first, was obvious to both horse and rider. Socks knew he was using his muscles more, stretching his limitations. So did Gerald. The young man was proud of the "improvement" in the colt. He had a false sense of pride in his training abilities. Based on the effects of a few drops of oil of mustard, Gerald felt that he had taught this horse how to use his legs more.

Socks had been easy to start, though the process seemed unnecessarily rough to him at times. He took to saddle and bridle with minimal fuss. Like most of his breed, he possessed a quiet, mostly agreeable, disposition. He had only truly tried to buck and dislodge his rider a few times, and at least one of those times, it was young Gerald's fault for being too rough and spurring Socks when there was no need to. He didn't terribly mind the light chains or rollers that were put on his forelegs as training devices. They were kind of bothersome at first, but didn't really hurt him until they were used in conjunction with the oil of mustard. The colt enjoyed the opportunity to get out of his stall, to get some exercise, to learn something new. He liked people. But something just wasn't right.

That oil of mustard was burning holes in his feet. At least that's how it felt. The chains and rollers were getting bigger and heavier. What had he done to deserve such treatment?

The next time they sored him, he put up a fight, but he still did what they wanted. He was lifting his front feet higher and driving more behind. Gerald and his boss, Ellis Walsh, put a twitch on the tip of Socks' nose while they used the eyedropper to apply the oil of mustard. Poor Socks was beginning to realize why his mama and the other mares had spoken of soring with such trepidation. He wondered how long he was going to be subjected to this. Was this to be his sentence for the rest of his life, or was there something he could do to make it all go away? He was soon given the answer to these questions, and would later realize what a lucky horse he was.

Even though young Socks was naturally talented, and a very handsome colt, in the mind of Ellis Walsh he wasn't the hottest prospect in the barn. Some of the other horses were responding to training better. And as is usually the case in a barn full of horses, they are almost all for sale, if the price is right.

Around Celebration time, in late August, a trainer from California came to Socks' barn with some of his customers. They were looking for a young show prospect. Ellis Walsh knew he couldn't show this trainer from California just any horse. If he showed him one he had just fixed, or one that was too sore, the man would probably walk out and he might not come back.

You see, this trainer from California was from the old school. He still believed in and practiced the "old way" of training, without chemicals. He had started out working for S.W. Beech and later, Winston Wiser, shortly after World War II. As a young man just out of the Marine Corp, he had even ridden Midnight Sun and Merry Go Boy on occasion. He had learned how to train Walking Horses before the use of chemicals came in fashion, before soring was invented.

Ellis rode a blue roan mare that moved the way the people from California liked. But her front feet were really scarred up from the mustard oil, and when her bell boots were removed, the West Coasters visibly grimaced. The scar rule was more strictly enforced out west than in Middle Tennessee. They would never be able to get the mare past inspection. This trainer and his customers would be embarrassed to have such a badly scarred animal in their barn, even though they liked almost everything else about her.

Socks came out next and the California trainer noticed right off that the colt had minimal scarring. With the big show coming up, Ellis and his assistants had been concentrating on other horses and had not ridden Socks much in the past few weeks. He had been started late, and to be honest, Ellis Walsh wasn't all too sure that Socks had what it takes to make a top show horse. He had begun to think of the colt as more of a good pleasure horse instead, and had backed off his training and soring of the colt.

Ellis had a pair of heavy steel trotting balls or rollers placed around Socks' front ankles and rode him up and down the barn aisle a few times. The colt started out pacey, then reached for a trot. In between he hit something the trainer from California really liked. He could tell the young gelding was green, but that didn't bother him at all. In fact, he liked the idea of developing the talent he thought he saw in the horse. Ellis stopped Socks in the middle of the barn and after sharing a somewhat off-color joke with the visitors, he got down and adjusted the stirrups to accommodate the tall man from California.

The strange man said a few soothing words to Socks and adjusted the curb chain before stepping into the saddle. He asked Gerald to remove the heavy trotting balls and replace them with a lighter pair. He also asked Ellis if it would be all right to ride Socks outside the barn. He knew there was a good straightaway along the north fence.

Ellis Walsh had no problem granting the Californian's requests. He knew the man was seriously interested in Socks, and he had respect for the man. After all, the two of them went way back. Ellis was just slightly the younger of the two, and he too had started out working for S.W. back in the late 1940's.

By the time soring came along in the mid-fifties, Royal "Roy" Riggins had already moved back to California and was winning at horse shows up and down the coast. He won the Pacific Coast Championship in 1950 on a three-year old son of Merry Go Boy. He'd seen the colt running out in pasture at Beech's place the year before, told the father of his bride about the horse, and they bought him and brought him to the family farm in Northern California.

Royal and his father-in-law formed a close bond and working relationship based, in part, on their mutual love for this wonderful breed of horse. Together, they brought to California some of the finest Walking Horses to come from Tennessee after the war.

It was a good time then; a time of growth, of optimism. World War II was over, as was the depression that preceded it. It was a brand new world, a new country. There was excitement in the air. The economy boomed. People had leisure time, money to buy horses, time to go to horse shows. Other than the fact that we were about to become involved in another armed conflict overseas, it was a good time for the country and a good time for the horse industry.

People at the fairs and horse shows packed the stands to watch the exciting Tennessee Walking Horses perform and compete. On the West Coast, they could always count on the tall, handsome man from northern California to put on a good show. He rode tall in the saddle with a smooth, effortless ease that was a joy to watch. His horses performed for the man on their back and for the crowd.

It was not unusual for trainers and horseman from other breeds to crowd the rail to watch Roy Riggins show a horse. It was obvious he had their admiration and respect. Even those in his own breed, whom he so often beat in competition, knew he had something special. The young man had found his niche, had found what he'd been born to do.

Born in Oklahoma in 1920, Royal Riggins was the son of a tenant farmer who had a knack for handling mules and horses. Back then, in Cotton County, there were few cars and trucks and no paved roads. Quite often when someone got their wagon, or truck, or Model A stuck, they would call on Royal's daddy to come pull them out with his little pair of mules. Called Sara and Jessie, his mules were small in stature but big in heart, and they would do anything for Curley Riggins. Curley wasn't a betting man but others who were had won more than one wager concerning the pulling power of those two mules.

One time that money changed hands, however, the mules weren't even involved. A farmer got his wagon stuck in some mud by the side of the road. The wagon was loaded with cotton and his big pair of horses couldn't budge it, no matter how much he whipped and cursed them.

They were in line to get their cotton weighed and a crowd had gathered. Someone in the crowd went down the line and asked Curley if he could help. After looking over the situation, Curley said he thought those big ol' horses ought to be able to pull that wagon out. Would anybody mind if he gave it a try? The murmur in the crowd was two-sided. A few wagers were made. The owner of the wagon just threw up his hands, and with a rather incredulous look, said:

"Have at it, I'm about ready to shoot the both of them."

Curley had one request, that the owner unhitch the team. This request was granted with another unbelieving smirk thrown toward the audience. Curley took the lines and walked the pair of sweating and stressed animals around a bit, talking to them all the while in a soothing manner. He turned them left and right, stopped, started, let them feel his hands through the lines, let them sense his confidence in their ability.

After a few minutes of getting acquainted and letting the horses calm down and catch their breath, Curley Riggins hitched the two horses back to the wagon, said a few more words to them and patted them on the shoulders. Then he took up the lines and stood behind the horses and to the side of the wagon. He declined the offer of the horsewhip without averting his attention from the two big horses and the task at hand.

He tapped both horses on the rump with the lines and clucked to them as he took up just enough slack for them to feel him in their mouths. Curley used his hands to tell the team that he wasn't going to hurt them and that he needed them to pull. They trusted this man and they understood what he was telling them through the lines. He had convinced the horses that they wanted to do what he wanted them to do. They leaned into their harness and pulled as hard as they could, and out came the wagon.

A cheer went up from the crowd and the owner of the team was shaking Curley's hand while shaking his own head in disbelief and smiling with gratitude. Little Royal was mighty proud of his daddy that day, and through the years, he watched and listened and learned a lot from the way his father handled his animals. From that day on, he understood the importance of communicating to horse or mule with his hands, and of gaining their trust. What goes through those reins or lines to the animal's mouth is more important than any gimmick in the world. It's not so much the tools you use, but how you use them, that really counts. A little patience and a good heart, along with a firm hand, will always accomplish more than brute force when it comes to working with animals. Curley Riggins instilled these principles in his son's mind through both words and actions.

The tall man from California had inherited his father's ability to understand and communicate in a special way with some of God's four-legged creatures. Socks was experiencing that now.

Royal Riggins walked Socks outside the barn. Then, with his legs and through the reins with his hands, he urged the colt on. He rode him through the pacey-ness and caught him before he got too trotty. Socks could feel him establishing a rhythm in his mouth with the reins that was somehow telling the horse's brain what the man wanted his body to do. Socks had experienced this with Ellis, and even with Gerald to some extent, but somehow this was different. This trainer from California had something special. His hands were firm, but gentle, and if he had to explain his movements and cues to someone in an analytical way, it would be hard for him. This came naturally to Royal Riggins; he was such a natural horseman that it was more a matter of subconscious effort, almost telepathy with the horse, than a series of well thought out promptings.

The weather this time of year in Middle Tennessee is predictably unpredictable. It was muggy and overcast. A thunderstorm could develop at any moment. Thunder was heard in the distance and the people and the horses could feel the tension of the gathering storm. Socks had not been ridden much in the past weeks, especially outside the barn. He was 'feeling his oats' a bit, as people like to say.

Half way through their second pass down the straightaway, a close bolt of lightening flashed to the west accompanied by an extremely loud clap of thunder. Socks jumped and as Roy headed him towards the barn he swelled up and hit a lick like he never had before. Socks felt like he was going to jump out of his skin but Roy Riggins kept him under control and collected and helped the colt channel this new energy and excitement into more leg motion. He was shaking his head and really walking. Roy could feel the colt using his shoulders more and really striding behind, like he should.

The people watching who knew Socks were surprised to see him look this good, although he was going a little faster than they liked. At that very moment, Roy realized he and the colt might be showing off a bit. If he got Socks looking too good, the price might go up. So, he stopped and dismounted, scratched Socks underneath the bridle where he somehow knew the colt had an itch, and handed the reins to Gerald, who led the young gelding into the barn.

The year was 1969, and that night Royal Riggins and his clients watched The Senator win the World Grand Championship at the Celebration in Shelbyville. It was storming in earnest by then, and at times it was raining so hard you could barely see the horses on the other side of the show ring. But The Senator was a mudder, at least he became one that night, and he won the big stake despite the downpour and the controversy.

The controversy and tension were there in a big way that night. Rumors were flying. It was rumored that The Senator's rider was packing a gun, and the friction between a group of trainers and the government men was at the boiling point. After all, this was the South, and these good ol' boys didn't take kindly to government men telling them what to do. They never had and never will. Whether it was running shine or soring horses, people around here were used to doing things their own way. This particular night, in the middle of dry Bedford County, there was plenty of evidence of both moonshine and oil of mustard.

Roy Riggins spent part of the evening sitting and talking with his old friend, French Brantley. As usual, they talked a lot about old times and how things had changed. Both of them had seen the Walking Horse business change tremendously, especially Mr. Brantley.

He loved to talk about great horses of the past and how they would compare with the horses of the present day. Of course, the gait had changed an awful lot in the last fifteen years, and some of the horses were now so man-made that it was hard to tell how they would do without the chemicals and the heavy shoes and pads on their front feet. But French Brantley still loved a good horse and he sure loved this breed. He was a huge supporter of the breed that had played such a big part in his life and in that of his family.

It was the Brantleys, after all, who had stood both Allan F-1 and Roan Allen F-38, two of the great foundation sires of the breed. Mr. Brantley knew that Royal Riggins was a special talent and that he was one of the few who still believed in the old way of training. Although they saw each other infrequently, the old man's face would always light up when he saw the tall Californian. It was as if he recognized a kindred spirit.

Mr. Brantley was always careful not to outwardly condemn what was happening to his coveted breed but he could never condone it either, especially to Royal. When the two of them talked he spoke longingly of the old days, the old horses, and the old way of going. Like many of the old-timers, French Brantley realized that this new, more animated gait of the Tennessee

Walking Horse was exciting for people to watch and was most likely here to stay. But he also felt that it was a dangerous direction to be going in and, if taken too far, could ruin everything. Deep down, they both knew the use of oil of mustard and other painful gimmicks to train a horse was just plain wrong. It wasn't natural, it was dishonest, and it was cruel to the horse.

Most of the trainers and exhibitors from Roy Riggins' era who had been in the Walking Horse business since the forties or before eventually went along with the new training methods. They had to, to compete, to have any chance of winning, to stay in business. At least that's what they told themselves, how they rationalized their abuse of these animals.

Royal was somewhat of a dinosaur for not going along with everybody else. He hated the sight of a sore horse. He would not tolerate it if he had any control over the situation. He had been asked to judge the Walking Horse classes at the Missouri State Fair a few years before and right up front he told the manager of the horse show that if a sore horse came in the ring he would send him right back out, without hesitation. Well, the manager was a good man and he liked the idea. The word spread. After Roy made good on his promise a time or two, they had the cleanest Walking Horse classes around. And Royal Riggins was asked to come back and judge the Missouri State Fair three more times in the years to come.

Royal was a man of conviction and he had come to his beliefs in his own unique way. In the middle 1950's, when soring came to be, he was told by his contemporaries what wonders a little drop of mustard oil could do to enhance a horse's gait.

By this point in time, Roy Riggins had already made a name for himself on the West Coast by winning consistently at the major shows. At first, he hesitated trying the chemical assistant. But he was a very competitive man and he didn't like the idea of his competitors having an unfair edge in the show ring. So, on his way back from Tennessee one year, along with a country ham and two Tennessee Faintin' Goats, he brought a couple bottles of oil of mustard.

The results were immediate. It didn't take much of the caustic chemical to get a reaction. The horses started reaching and squatting more behind, and lifting and reaching more with their front legs. It squared up some of the pacier horses. But the negative results were immediate as well, and Royal noticed the horses moved more slowly going in and out of their stalls. They were in pain, and he knew it.

The mustard oil blistered the area it was applied to, and this blister could very easily become raw, oozing blood and puss, and eventually leave a very ugly and permanent scar. From the beginning, Roy had felt some qualms about using this chemical to help him train his horses. With each day, he became more and more uncomfortable with what he was doing.

Training and showing Walking Horses had evolved quite a bit by this time. Over the ten years or so that Roy Riggins had been involved with the breed, trainers had found that letting the front feet grow longer and adding some leather padding between the hoof and the shoe enhanced the horse's gait. But this had no negative effect on the horse that Royal could see and he had no qualms at all about making a horse a little taller in front. As long as it was done gradually and at the correct angle, and not taken to an extreme, he knew this could never really hurt a horse.

One morning, as Roy came in on a pretty bay mare, Big Jim hollered at him from one of the stalls. The trainer dismounted, put the mare in the crossties, and went to see what the fuss was about. It was the black colt, the big three year-old by Midnight Sun. He was lying down, and every once in a while, letting out a low moan or groan.

Big Jim said; "Can't get him up, Roy. Might be colic."

That had been Royal's first thought. But he wasn't so sure.

They dragged the big colt to his feet, with a little persuasion from the riding crop, and got him out of the stall and into the barn aisle. If it was colic, they had to keep the colt on his feet and moving. For some reason, Roy felt that the colt was more concerned about pain in his front feet than in his stomach. He could tell by the way he moved. When he told Big Jim what he was thinking, Jim said; "Maybe I put a little too much on him this morning."

Roy stared at Big Jim and said; "You fixed him too? I just put a couple drops on him a little while ago, myself. Look at him. This colt can barely walk!"

Royal Riggins just stood there for a few minutes contemplating the dirt of the barn aisle. Then he jerked his head up and said:

"I can't do this anymore! That's it! Jimbo, after you wash this colt's legs real good, put some of that green salve on him. Then I want you to take those bottles of mustard oil and throw them in the trash. I never want to see any sign of that stuff in my barn again! Never!"

THREE

The week after The Senator won the Tennessee Walking Horse World Grand Championship, Socks was loaded up and shipped to California to begin a new life. When Socks arrived in California, Royal Riggins' barn was the most successful Walking Horse facility on the West Coast. Roy had recently moved his operation from the L.A. County fairgrounds in Pomona to a beautiful setting in the Chino Hills. The entire ranch was huge, spanning some three thousand acres. The barn, which was to be Socks' new home, was built in 1922 by a Chicago banker for his imported Arabian horses. South American mahogany had been brought in to build this magnificent structure. The aisle was wide and long, similar to the Walsh barn in Tennessee, but slightly wider. On bad weather days, horses were worked in the ample space inside the barn. Roy Riggins preferred to work the horses outside, though, either in the ring or down the eucalyptus lined straightaway, or up the slight incline of one of the surrounding, rolling hills.

As Socks got used to his new surroundings, he noticed more

differences between this barn and his former home. For one, he never caught a whiff of that awful oil of mustard. Early one morning he thought he did but it was as he was awakening from a bad dream and he soon realized the odor he thought he smelled was just part of his memory or dream.

Music was constantly playing from the dusty old radio that sat precariously on a plywood shelf next to the tack room door. The music was mostly country and it seemed like someone was almost always singing along. The people were happy and so were the horses. Socks knew he was happier here. With each day the burden of his life felt a little lighter and the memory of the oil of mustard became more and more distant.

The Walsh Farm in Tennessee had not been total gloom and doom. Ellis Walsh always had a lot of people around and he kept them laughing a good portion of the time. He was a very outgoing person, a frequent joke teller, and quite a prankster. Socks was an optimistic horse, as was most of his breed, and he tried to enjoy life no matter what the circumstances. But at his old home there was always an underlying darkness.

Here in California, the day began early with alfalfa pellets and a little sweet feed. Then, as Royal's son Ricky and the Mexican they called Rodriguez cleaned stalls, horses were selected for work. Socks knew when it was about to be his turn. He usually came up after Margie, the pretty dark chestnut mare with the flaxen mane and tail. Margie was stabled across from him and down a couple stalls.

Socks could always tell when Big Jim went to get her because all the stallions in the barn took notice and stirred in their stalls. Some of them called out in low, sexy voices that Margie pretended not to hear. The big bald-faced colt next to him made a particular fool of himself, ranting and raving, huffing and puffing, stomping and pacing the stall. Socks was actually embarrassed for him sometimes. The horse had too few brains, and way too many hormones, as far as he was concerned.

Socks looked forward to his daily workouts. It was nice to get outside and get some exercise. Back in Tennessee, under Ellis Walsh's tutelage, Socks had rarely been worked outside the barn and had never been ridden six days a week for any length of time that he could remember. Ellis had learned as Roy Riggins had, from the old school, but he had gradually slipped into the habit of letting the chemicals do most of the work.

The rolling hills of southern California were mostly green in the winter and brown in the summer, another opposite of Tennessee. Socks kept thinking he might see some snow that winter, though he wasn't sure it ever seemed quite cold enough. Not cold enough to snow maybe, but it still got cold. On the mornings Socks could see his breath, he couldn't wait to get outside and stretch his legs. Roy usually worked Socks with a pair of light wooden rattlers, or "trotting balls" strapped below his ankles. He sometimes used the leather bell-boots that he would show the colt in. The trainer always wore at least one short, English spur. He didn't use that spur much but Socks was always aware of where it was.

Socks' gait improved almost daily. Since he no longer felt that awful sting from the mustard oil, the horse moved free and easy, more naturally, and with more speed. Through the repetitive workouts his trainer was teaching Socks how to look his best. Royal liked to ride him on, pushing him to use his front end more, but he was careful not to take him too fast to where he might shorten up behind.

He knew Socks' strong point was his back end, the way his hind legs reached up underneath his body when he walked. He had a tremendous overstride, the distance that his hind hoof overstepped the placement of his corresponding front hoof. The horse also had a lot of natural head motion and showiness about him. Roy just wanted him to do a little more with his front legs without sacrificing any back end. He knew the judges would be impressed by Socks' pure beauty and true, natural walk.

Socks knew Roy was trying to get him to do more. He could feel the man's urging. The colt felt Royal's legs push him on, but not too fast. It wasn't speed he was asking for, it was more action. He did this by pushing Socks up into the bridle and keeping him collected without getting too heavy handed. Other riders who rode Riggins trained horses always noticed and often commented on how light their mouths were.

The trainer worked Socks a lot at a speed somewhere between a flat-walk and a running walk. This gave him the best of both worlds, and kept Socks from getting too lazy in the slower gait. He would sometimes take Socks out across a field or up a slight incline or purposely ride the colt over uneven ground, watching out for squirrel holes, of course. This helped square the colt up and made him work a little harder. The bit he used was a mild, broken mouth-piece bit with a short shank and curb chain.

One morning not long after arriving in California the trainer turned Socks' head to the rail, pressed him with his heel, leaned forward slightly and before Socks knew what he was doing, he found himself loping around the ring. His trainers back in Tennessee had never cantered Socks. He guessed they just never got around to it. As usual, Roy kept the colt collected, didn't let him run off or get all strung out. Socks wanted to go a little too fast at first but that was normal and the trainer gradually slowed him and calmed him down.

Before long, cantering was old hat for Socks. He took to it very well, better than most. Roy liked the young gelding's attitude. He seemed to want to work and was a quick learner. The trainer had an ulterior motive for teaching Socks to canter early on. He felt it might aid in trying to get the colt to break loose in front. It would help Socks to use his shoulders more.

Besides the obnoxious bald-faced young stallion on his left,

Socks was stabled next to a pretty bay mare they called Lacey. What a sweetheart. Even though Socks had been gelded at a young age, he could still be attracted to a pretty mare. He didn't get all breathy and sweaty like young Baldy, but he felt an immediate attraction for Lacey that grew deeper with time.

When Socks was first put in the stall between Baldy and Lacey, he was sort of in shock from the long road trip and the unfamiliar surroundings. As he got his bearings, he first tried to warm up to the bald-faced colt. Though they were close in age, Socks soon found out he had little in common with the young stallion. Baldy's hormones had kicked in in a big way already, and he could hardly think of anything else. Socks soon found that he had more in common with the pretty, quiet bay mare on the other side.

Lacey was more than six years older than Socks and had been born and raised in Tennessee. Socks didn't realize it at first, but she reminded him of his mother. The bay mare and Socks were both of double Midnight Sun breeding meaning Midnight Sun was their grandsire on both sides. Socks found these things out in one of his conversations with her. Lacey was generally a quiet mare but once she got hold of a subject, she liked to stick with it. She was very informative. In that way too, she reminded Socks of his mother.

Socks even found out a little bit about his father from his new friend. His ears perked up one day as Lacey said:

"You know, Socks, I met your daddy a while back. Not in Tennessee, but out here in California. Of course, I'd heard a lot about him, but had never seen him in person. Well, one day he just shows up at our barn with his trainer. It was wintertime, right before the Rose Parade. Sometimes horses would stay at our barn for the day or two before the parade, then, trailer over to it in the middle of the night. That was when we were still at the Fairgrounds in Pomona.

"When your daddy arrived from Tennessee, it was after he had won the World Grand Championship. Let me tell you, my young friend, your sire is one magnificent animal. He is very, very good looking. Of course he knows it, but that's all right.

"He was pretty tired from his trip, like you were, but he was also restless. When they brought him out of his stall to fit him with his rubber shoes, he was snorting and showing off a bit. He was flirting, too. He looked me right in the eye a couple times, and I thought I was going to melt.

"The men put the rubber shoes on him to make it easier on him in the parade over those hard, slick, city streets. When they were finished, your daddy let his trainer get on him and ride up and down the barn aisle a few times. Now Socks, I don't know if they fixed him that day or not but the way he moved I could certainly see why he was the World's Champion.

"I'm sure he had seen plenty of mustard oil in his career. I could see the scars. I could also see that the horse had an abundance of natural ability. I really think they kept him pretty clean for his trip to the Rose Parade. I just loved watching him strut up and down our barn aisle. His trainer seemed to be totally in tune with what your daddy was doing.

"They didn't work your daddy long, just enough to loosen him up a bit. With the Rose Parade the next day he would be getting plenty of exercise, believe me. Before they put Sun's Delight back in his stall our trainer got to ride him for a few passes. It seemed to me that Roy and the man who rode your sire had known each other a long time. Now I know I may be prejudiced, Socks, but I love the way Royal Riggins sits a horse. I may have imagined it, but I thought I saw your daddy swell up just a little more when Roy did his thing and rode him on a bit."

Socks couldn't believe it! Royal Riggins, his new trainer, had actually ridden Socks' own sire a few years ago right here in Southern California! Briefly, but still, the same man that got on

Socks each day now had at one time picked up the reins and thrown a leg over his daddy's back. Who woulda thought? It made him feel proud and helped him connect even more with the man that was now his trainer.

This wouldn't be such a big deal to a lot of horses. But Socks was so in love with the ancestry and lore of his breed that this made quite an impression on him. It was a cosmic connection, a link to the past. He knew his mama would understand how he was feeling and he thought Lacey did, as well. In fact, that's probably why she told him the story to begin with.

When Socks wasn't scouring the floor of his stall for some fallen alfalfa pellet or morsel of sweet feed he might have missed, or taking a nap, he liked to watch the other horses being worked. Sometimes he and Lacey would watch together and comment about what was going on.

"Mr. Riggins sure has a lot of patience with young Baldy, doesn't he? He's been ground driving him for several days now and the colt still has to act stupid half the time."

"That's true Socks. He acts stupid here in the barn where the poor colt is distracted by every stall with a female in it. But I can see outside, where Roy is working Baldy in the little ring, and it looks like his patience is paying off. The colt actually settles down a bit and starts paying attention to his trainer, doing what he's supposed to do. Roy has him turning well, stopping, starting, and even backing and doing a well-collected little walk. The colt is really not all that bad when he puts his mind to his work."

"I wonder why I never was ground driven when I was being started, Miss Lacey? After they put a saddle and bridle on me in the stall a couple of times, one day Gerald just got on me and started ridin'. They closed the barn doors, led me out into the middle of the aisle and then held me, one man on each side, as Gerald got up. He took his time gettin' all the way up of course, 'cause I wasn't all too keen on having his weight on my back at first.

"Once he got up there in the middle of my back, the other men started leading me around the barn, gradually backin' off but watching me real close. Gerald was pullin' that snaffle bit from one side to the other, teaching me to turn. Every once in a while he would pull back, and kinda seesaw the reins and say 'whoa.' I remember how the bit rubbed sores on both sides of my mouth, and the men never put any medicine on 'em. They just scabbed over, then rubbed raw again the next time they rode me. Eventually, the man on my right side went away and just the one on my left was leading me around. He let his lead rope out farther and farther until 'fore long it was just me and Gerald out there walking around the barn aisle."

"Did you buck?"

"Oh, I guess I started to a couple times. But Gerald kept my head up most the time and I didn't really mind him being up there all that much, though he could have been a little nicer about it. Now, some of the other colts, a couple come to mind, they knew how to buck. They weren't too shy about it, either. Seemed like it came to 'em naturally. Did you buck when you were started, Miss Lacey?"

"Well now, that was a few seasons back you know. But, if I remember right, I bucked and bucked like I was born to it. I threw that boy that was trying to ride me twice before they twitched my nose and I decided to let him stay on my back a while."

"Why, Miss Lacey that does not sound like you. You're so quiet and polite, such a fine southern lady, if I do say so."

"Well thank you, Socks. But, I was a hot young filly with a little bit of an attitude back then. The men that started me didn't have the patience or the horse sense of a Royal Riggins. They were way too rough. They didn't have the smarts to ground drive me for a while before they got on my back.

"I heard Roy tell somebody one time how he learned a lot

about patience and the importance of ground work from a man named Doc Young. Doc was a Saddlebred trainer who used to be stabled next to him at the fairgrounds. According to Royal Riggins, he could get a horse to slow-gait, or trot practically in place, if he wanted to. Roy said ol' Doc could talk to his horses right through those lines like they were telephone wires. Now, he might be exaggerating a bit, but it's true that there are all different kinds of horse trainers out there, Socks. The way I was started they rushed me, they took short cuts like they were in a hurry for some reason. They sored me right away too, like they did you. I was not happy so I acted out. It wasn't my fault."

"Did you hurt anyone?"

"No, I didn't hurt anyone, but I can't say I didn't want to. Socks, as time goes by and as you get around more and talk to horses that have been around more, you will realize how fortunate we are to be right where we are. We are being trained by an honest, talented, horse loving man, who knows more about how to communicate with horses and how to treat them right, than a whole herd of those other guys."

FOUR

Before Junior's first show, he had to be conditioned for inspection. The DQP's, or Designated Qualified Persons as the inspectors are called, would be rubbing and probing each horse's pastern area looking for over-sensitivity, or soreness, which would disqualify the horse from competition, in theory. However, the DQP's are hired by the Tennessee Walking Horse Exhibitors Association, through its National Horse Show Commission, in conjunction with the USDA. Their salaries are paid, in part, by the very industry they are supposed to be monitoring.

"Kinda like the fox guardin' the chicken coop," was how Old Timer put it.

Still, both the inspectors and the exhibitors try very hard to project an appearance of propriety, even though they all know what has been done to these show horses for them to be able to compete.

"They are all sore. It's just a matter of degrees," said Old Timer when Junior got back in his stall after Jeremy and Sammy Lee had put him through a mock inspection.

One of the men held the colt with the chain of the lead shank under Junior's lip, where he would feel it bite should he flinch. The other man approached Junior and ran his hand down one of the colt's front legs, squeezing and pushing with his fingers below the horse's ankle. The man pressed along the coronet band at the top of the hoof, then picked up Junior's foot and began pressing his thumbs into the hollow at the back of the pastern. Junior pulled back in pain and Jeremy jerked down on the chain while Sammy beat the colt with a baseball bat. This oft-repeated procedure eventually convinced Junior to stand still during such tests, beat into submission. The men called this "stewarding" a horse, teaching him or her not to flinch, not to move at all when being handled by the inspection stewards.

"You see, Junior." Old Timer explained. "These, what they call DQP's, have been trained to 'inspect' in a certain way, follow a specific procedure, which makes it easy for Mr. Sammy and Jeremy to anticipate what they will do. They know if they can get you to behave yourself in this here pretend inspection, then, you'll most likely do well at the show 'cause they know there won't be no surprises. The inspectors know you're sore. They know you're trained with chemicals and pressure shoeing but that's not the issue. Truth is not the issue. It's whether or not you can pass the prescribed criteria.

"Besides, they've always got their ace in the hole. It's called Hurricane Spray. It's got lydocaine in it, so it temporarily numbs your legs long enough for you to get through inspection. Then, when it wears off, look out! Here comes the hurt again.

"See, Junior, where there's a will there's a way, unfortunately. Believe you me those inspectors don't want to see you flinch either. They want the show to go on just as much as the trainers and exhibitors do. It's their bread and butter. Why, if they was to turn back every sore horse at the show, there wouldn't be any show now would there? Oh, once in a while they'll turn one back, write somebody up, but that's all part of the scam.

"They'll make an example of someone to make it look like they're doin' their job. Then the horse they write up won't be able to show for a while, and the trainer and the owners might be fined a few thousand dollars or even suspended from showing for a few months. But that doesn't really hurt 'em. All the top trainers have been fined and, or, suspended at some time or other. They're all still in business, doin' what they do, doin' what they're doin' to you, and makin' lots of money at it."

"I don't understand. If it's against the law to hurt us like this, how can these people keep getting away with it? Doesn't anybody care?"

"Oh, there's plenty of people who care, Junior. I know that for a fact. I've known people in my own life who cared plenty. Some of them have tried to stop this whole darn thing, tried for years. They've had their little victories here and there where it looks like they might be gettin' somewhere. But the bad guys keep comin' out on top. They keep comin' up with new ways to cheat, new ways to lie, to cover things up.

"It's like a big ol' dirty snowball rollin' down hill. The longer they get away with it, the harder it is to stop. Good people can try to stop it. And, they may chip away at it from time to time. But, that ball of snow will just patch itself up and keep on rollin' down hill, headed straight to hell, without so much as slowin' down.

"You see, Junior, it's all about money. This here Walking Horse business is a billion dollar industry. And, in the human way of thinking, money talks. Most times, money talks a lot louder than the voice of truth or honesty. It don't seem right, but that's the way it is.

"There are lots of people makin' lots of money in this business, raising families, buying nice farms and houses and trucks and trailers and fancy cars. It doesn't matter to them that this whole industry is based on a lie. They see the results, the kind of life it brings them. The notoriety, the fame from winnin' championships, all that clouds their judgment, allows them to rationalize. Then, I guess there's some of 'em that are just plain mean and couldn't care less how much they hurt their animals.

"Well, guess I ought to get off my soapbox for a while and get back to tellin' you more about the history of our breed. That's what I love talking about more than anything. Probably because I'm so old and have lived through a lot of it and heard about so much. Not much I can do now except talk about it. I guess I'm kinda historical, myself, Junior. I said historical, now. Don't be surprised if you hear me jumpin' back on that soapbox now and then. 'Cause that is one thing I can still get pretty worked up about, Junior. No doubt about it.

"You remember I told you about some of our ancestors that was involved in the war between the Gray and the Blue. Well, after that war, some things never were the same. Nevertheless, life around here eventually got somewhat back to normal, whatever that is. Without the horror of the war hanging over their heads, people could concentrate a little more on their horse raisin'.

"One of the great sires around here after the war was Boone's Grey John. He was still inside his mama when, toward the end of the war, a group of Blue men dropped her off at Nathaniel Boone's place. I guess she was having a hard time keepin' up with them 'cause she was so close to having her young 'un, so they just dropped her off there and took one of Boone's younger horses to replace her. Now, Captain Boone was not real happy about the swap when he first got home and saw this northern mare and her spindly little blue roan colt. But, the mare was a nice mare, and the colt grew on him as he grew up. He got lighter in color, too. So they called him Grey John.

"Captain Boone liked him even more when he started ridin' the colt. Word spread quickly about Grey John's flashy gaits and speed. Before long, people were bringing their mares from far and wide to breed to this stallion of Nathaniel Boone's. It's too bad we don't know more about his ancestry, Junior.

"Ol' Grey John became quite a breedin' horse. He stood at Booneville until he was an old horse. Not as old as me, of course, but he was in his twenties. Then, after a season out around Petersburg, he went on to Bedford County, where he stood for the last few years of his life. That last move would prove real important to ol' Grey John. Important to the rest of us, too.

"See, there was another prominent stallion of that period in Bedford County, Tennessee. He also came from northern bloodlines. 'Cept, it wasn't his mama got left behind, like Boone's Grey John, it was his granddaddy.

"There was this blacksmith over in Warner's Bridge, just northwest of Shelbyville. His name was Mike Earnhart and he was neutral in the war. Guess he figured that way he could shoe horses for both sides and make a livin' without getting shot. Anyhow, one day a certain Blue general rides up on a very worn-out stallion. He figures this horse can't go no further, so he leaves him with Mike Earnhart, and takes off on another horse. Even swap.

"This tired ol' stud horse was named Old Driver, and Earnhart bred him to a young mare he had, givin' her a stud colt they called Young Driver. Later on, a mare by Brown Pilot was bred to Young Driver and out came a beautiful dark bay stallion they named Earnhart's Brooks.

"Earnhart's Brooks is the horse I'm talking about, Junior. As soon as he was old enough, they started breedin' mares to him, and in no time at all he won wide acclaim as a great sire. One of his colts, Rattler Brooks, paced a mile in a record two minutes twenty-three and a half seconds. He did that in October of 1888. Once, the old horse hisself did a fast runnin' walk around the public square in Shelbyville while the man on his back held a glass of water in his hand and didn't spill a drop. This was done, of course, to win a small wager for his master.

"The rivalry in Bedford County between Earnhart's Brooks

and Boone's Grey John grew to mythical proportions. The northwestern part of the county became known as 'Earnhart's Brooks country' and the southeastern part was 'Grey John country.'

"Loyalties were strong on both sides and got to such a point that eventually someone came up with the idea of a competition between the two sires and their get. Not just a race, Junior, but a 'horse show'.

"In those days, horse shows were pretty rare in this part of the country with racing bein' the primary means of equine competition. So, this was quite an event. People turned out in a big way. They held it at the Bedford County Fairgrounds.

"At this here show, the two famous sires and their young 'uns were shown under saddle. Except for the ones that were too young to saddle up, of course. Now, they say that Earnhart's Brooks was a prettier, finer horse than ol' Grey John. Accordin' to some, he was better trained and more precise in his gaits. But Grey John, Junior, he was stronger and faster, clocked at a mile in eight minutes at the runnin' walk. And speed was still awful important in those days. Tradition has it, at least if you talk to Captain Boone's relatives, that Grey John and his get won the contest.

"Of course now, Junior, I'm sure there was plenty of contrary opinions out there as to just who did win that contest. Just like at the horse shows they have today. Everybody thinks their horse is best. Guess if they didn't, wouldn't be much need for a show, now would there?"

Junior had drifted off again, listening to the old one's stories. He found himself being ridden around a ring full of flat shod horses doing versions of an easygoing, low action, flat walk. There was an announcer with a megaphone. The crowd in the stands was alive with conversation. The men in top hats and the ladies with parasols were intent on the activity in the ring. As the faster gait was called, Junior felt his rider urging him on.

To Junior's surprise, he was able to step out quite easily. His front legs weren't reaching for the sky. They didn't burn with pain. He wasn't squatting behind. He was reaching forward with both front and hind legs in a coordinated four-beat walk. He was covering ground, too. Soon, he began to pass other horses. This was fun. Junior felt like he was flying. He could beat these other horses. He knew he could.

The crowd began to follow Junior around the ring. He could hear them cheering, and some of them were calling his name. The stall door slid open and there stood Jeremy.

"Come on, Junior, quit dreaming."

"Back to reality", Junior told himself.

Jeremy led him to the wash rack and began to undo his leg wraps. His tailset and blanket were left alone. For some reason, he didn't quite know why, Junior had an uneasy feeling about what was about to happen.

Junior had been in training for several months now and though the chemicals used to sore him did much less outward damage than the straight oil of mustard used in the 50's and 60's, it was impossible to avoid some scarring and loss of hair. The Horse Protection Act, passed in 1970 with nothing but good intentions, was but a bump in the road for the very inventive Walking Horse trainers and owners bent on abusing their animals. It only spurred them to find new, more sophisticated soring methods, and more effective ways of covering their tracks.

Besides being inspected for signs of soreness prior to showing, horses competing in today's shows must adhere to the "scar rules". It is against USDA and horse show rules for horses to have visible bi-lateral scars or evidence of soring. Although these rules are enforced with the same "fox guarding the chicken coop" teamwork Old Timer talks about, there must be at least some semblance of true adherence to the rules.

In order to restore the hair to his pastern area, Junior was about to undergo a life-changing experience. He thought he had been hurt before, that he had endured severe pain. Well, that was nothing compared to what he was about to go through.

Jeremy clipped the hair on Junior's front legs from his ankle down to the coronet band and from front to back. Using the finest ear clippers, Jeremy made as close a cut as he could without drawing blood. William cleaned off the trimmed area with brush and towel while Jeremy donned a pair of industrial strength rubber gloves. Then the young man that Junior figured had been born mean began mixing a fine white powder with alcohol in a bowl he placed on the workbench. The combination of powder and liquid soon evolved into a thick white paste. When Jeremy felt he had just the right mixture, he applied the paste to the area of Junior's front legs that he had just clipped with a spatula. Before he wrapped the colt's legs in plastic wrap, Jeremy pressed and squeezed the pasty substance onto the skin with his still gloved hands.

The white powder used to make this paste was salicylic acid, which is used as a food preservative and in the preparation of aspirin. Sounds harmless enough, but in this application the pain is so severe that it is said to cause unconsciousness, and even death in some cases. When the men finished wrapping the colt's legs in plastic they returned him to his stall to suffer alone. In about three days, they would drag the colt out of his stall and carefully remove the plastic wrap. Then they would remove the hardened paste and dead skin using a common hair comb and much care. It would be similar to removing a scab. If you pulled too quickly you drew blood so they would be careful. The horse's legs remain sore for several more days after the procedure. Junior's pain increased beyond anything he had experienced before.

Junior was a big, strong colt. He had some sense of that. He was also highly intelligent and perhaps more sensitive than some of the other horses. He felt he had been through a lot already. His legs had been burned with a variety of chemical irritants since he began his training. He knew it was wrong. He wanted to fight back, to run away somehow, but he didn't know how.

Of all the things he had been through, he had not experienced anything like this before. That night, at feeding time, the men didn't even bother to put out feed for the colt. They knew he wouldn't be able to eat. William brought him a bucket of water the second day and held Junior's head up so he could get to it. He tried to drink, because he was dying of thirst, but he managed to do little more than wet his lips, he was in such agony. He would not, could not, stand for three days and nights. When he was finally able to stand, he had to be whipped and pulled to an upright position. This new pain had surpassed any threshold Junior was used to with the soring chemicals.

The pain was unbearable. He couldn't think straight. What was happening to him? What was he going to do? Who would help him? Could anyone help him?

Junior drifted off into a fitful mid-afternoon slumber. Not because he was tired or sleepy, but because his subconscious was a refuge from the pain. As a kind of defense mechanism, Junior fell moaning and sweating into the world of his dreams. These dreams, which at first had frightened him so, were becoming a welcome escape.

Once again, he was back on the battlefield. He was lying on his side. He raised his head to have a look around, and saw his motionless rider lying a few feet away. The noise of the battle was all around him. He could smell the powder, the burning flesh, the blood, the sweat. Though his legs were on fire, or felt like they were, Junior struggled to his feet. He noticed another riderless horse off to his left through the trees. This horse was joined by two other horses without riders. They were looking around and talking, as if trying to decide what to do.

The leader was a big Thoroughbred-looking stallion, a beautiful, muscular, red sorrel. Without really knowing what he was doing, or why, Junior went over to them. His front feet hurt something awful but he knew he had to do something.

Just then, a Blue rider rode up and took hold of Junior's reins, and those of the other horses. Two other Blue soldiers with other captured Gray horses joined them as they headed down the slope toward the setting sun. They soon left the cover of the trees and followed a well-worn path that turned northward.

With nightfall, the small party made camp. They were off the road and not far from the river. Junior could smell the water and realized how thirsty he was.

As the horses were picketed, Junior noticed the man who tied them up looked an awful lot like William. Then he looked at the other two men. It was Jeremy and Sammy Lee Belford in the other Blue uniforms.

The men drank coffee and talked and laughed while sitting around a campfire. Then they got up and approached the horses. William held Junior's head and Sammy Belford barked some orders while Jeremy pulled out a paintbrush and an old coffee can from somewhere. The "paint" spilling out of the can was dark blue in color. It had a horrific odor and Junior tried to pull back and strike. William had a hold of his left ear and was pulling down and twisting at the same time.

Jeremy managed to slop a large amount of the blue gunk on Junior's legs as the colt struggled. Plastic wrap appeared from nowhere, and soon Junior's legs were wrapped and he was left alone to stand between two locust trees.

Stunned at what had just happened to him, Junior stood with his head lowered and all four feet close together, a picture of total defeat and despair. He watched in detached melancholy as the other horses received their "treatments".

When they were finished with the horses, the men returned to the campfire, laughing. Junior shuddered as he heard Sammy Belford's loud, devilish laugh echo through the woods.

That laugh was still ringing in his head when one of the other horses edged over to him and whispered something about getting out of here, getting back to the Gray men. It was the big sorrel stallion.

"They call me 'The Traveler', Junior, nice to meet ya. I'm here to tell you we've got to get back to our own side before it's too late. We've got to get this blue stuff off our legs before it burns right through us. Before it stamps our souls.

"Heard tell, if you get painted enough times, as much as you hate it, you eventually get used to it. It's like being brainwashed. It becomes a part of your life. You accept it and what it does to you, even though you know it's wrong.

"That burning you feel that's the blue trying to get through. It's going to burn and burn, hotter and hotter, till you give in to it, Junior. Believe me, I know.

"It won't be easy, Son, but you've got to fight it. Fight it now, while you still can. You can do it. I know you can. You're special. We've been watching you. You're one of us. You're a survivor."

A handsome bay stallion appeared from nowhere and untied his tether. The next thing Junior knew, he was racing down the dirt road with a handful of other horses. The blue goop that had been painted on his legs turned a blue-green then a yellow color, then finally to blood red. It burned like hell.

Though he felt like he was racing Junior realized he was doing a slow, very animated, sore-legged running walk. He was squatting behind with his hocks almost touching the ground. He was reaching for the sky with his front legs. He wanted to go faster but he couldn't.

He felt as if he couldn't get any traction, like he was spinning his wheels and not going anywhere. The farther he went, though, and the more determined he was to escape, the faster he was able to go. He began picking up speed as some of the bloody chemical on his legs was thrown off with every step. Soon, the pads and lead and heavy shoes were being tossed from his feet.

Traveler ran beside him for a moment, urging him on. Then, the big sorrel took the lead again heading them toward the river. The group of escaping horses turned left and took off across an open field, the Blue men in hot pursuit.

"When you get to the river swim to the other side! You'll be safe there."

It was Traveler's voice, winded and urgent.

Junior looked back over his shoulder and saw Sammy Lee, sword in hand, a fearsome, evil, expression on his face. Behind him rode Jeremy and William. They were coming on fast. Junior hoped with all his might that he and the others would reach the river before the maniacs in blue caught up with them.

He lay in his stall for three days and three nights under the spell of the salicylic acid. His moans were audible, his fever high. The pain was unbelievable.

Old Timer witnessed his young friend's torment with anguish and frustration. He had seen this before but that did not diminish his anger at what was happening. If there was just something he could do! The old gelding knew he didn't have a whole lot of days left to him on this earth. If there was some way he could help he was determined to find it. He racked his brain for a way he could help his friend before it was too late.

Whether it was the knowledge of his own impending mortality, or the history of this breed he loved, or being eyewitness to the awful plight of someone he had grown to care about, Old Timer knew he had to do something, but what?

Meanwhile, Junior experienced more near-escapes in his increasingly vivid dreams. Each time, it was Traveler and his friends who came to his aid. They seemed to be expecting him. Each time they would end up racing for the river, trying to reach the other side, and safety. Junior felt as if these spirit-horses of his dreams were trying to teach him something, something he had a sense of but couldn't quite pin down.

FIVE

Junior won his first show without much competition. The second time he showed was at a small town southeast of Nashville. It took place at an elementary school near the edge of town. A temporary show ring was set up on the grass behind the school. A grandstand on one side and folding chairs around the ring accommodated the crowd.

Junior and three other horses from Sammy Belford's barn were hauled to the show in a six-horse, gooseneck trailer. When they arrived, they pulled in and parked between Tim Sutton and Mitchell Lenz. Tim had just been released from a six month showing suspension and Mitch was waiting to hear what his punishment would be following a recent infraction of USDA rules.

Sammy had been lucky the past couple of years with no serious violations on his record. Before that he had been suspended from showing for two whole years. Two years was a stiff penalty comparatively, but Sammy didn't let it slow him down. He worked out a deal with his buddy Mitch to show his horses for him.

He set Mitch up in a barn just down the road from the Belford farm and kept his business going. Mitch had been starting some colts for Sammy during this time, and though it seemed he had gone out on his own, he continued to work for Sammy Lee Belford. Mitch got to step into the limelight some and Sammy got to stay in business. The Belford customers were happy because they already knew Mitch, and they knew that Sammy was still involved in the training and showing of their horses. The trainers were once again showing their lack of concern and respect for government rules and sanctions. Since his reinstatement Sammy still sent some colts to Mitch, but the younger man had picked up some horses on his own, as well.

Tim Sutton was a second-generation Walking Horse trainer with a history of drug and alcohol abuse. Rumor has it that Tim would often snort cocaine before a class and just as often blow some up his horse's nose to give him an "edge". He had a black two-year-old stud colt he hoped was ready for the competition tonight. Tim had seen Junior work and knew he was the horse to beat.

The two-year-old stallion and gelding class was scheduled about midway through the evening program. One of the other horses in Junior's trailer had already been shown and was being cooled out, having brought back a blue ribbon, when Jeremy began to get Junior ready to show. Junior was tied to the outside of the trailer and kept shifting around to see what he could see. He was a little nervous but couldn't help it. This was only his second show.

The area where the trailers were parked was not well lighted, but Junior could see a few other horses tied to trailers. He could see some being led toward the show area and some being led back lathered with sweat. Horses nickered occasionally, but mostly he heard human voices. Some were low and conspiring, some were loud and boisterous, celebratory. Still others were angry and bitter. There was another sound Junior heard from almost every direction in the trailer area. It was the sound of aerosol spray.

The air this night was thick and muggy but not overly hot. Junior felt good except for his sore front feet. Jeremy put the saddle on and cinched up the girth snugly, but not too tight. He would tighten it later. It was time to take the colt up to the inspection station.

Jeremy shook the can and sprayed. He sprayed the lydocaine on Junior's front legs, all around. Then he pressed his fingers onto the front and back of the colt's pastern area. Jeremy stood back and Sammy took the can, shook it and sprayed some more. Better too much than too little. Then Sammy pressed his fingers where he knew the inspectors would press, to see if the horse flinched. Junior did not move.

The colt seemed ready. Time to be inspected. They led Junior towards the back of the grandstand where the DQP's had set up their place of inspection. As Sammy led the colt, Jeremy walked behind, clucking and occasionally letting Junior feel the sting of the riding crop he carried. Junior was walking too slowly. They stopped twice to rub and probe, making sure.

In spite of his slow, obviously sore walk, Junior passed the inspection with flying colors. He was led to a spot along the fence that enclosed the inspection and warm-up area where Ramon was waiting with the equipment cart. This cart held racks of different sized chains, Junior's tail brace, all kinds of ointments, lead weights, grooming tools and who knows what else.

The trainer got on the colt and "dog walked" him, then rode him on a bit for two passes down the middle of the inspection area. Everybody was watching, even the people who pretended not to.

This was the first or second show of the season, of their lives, for most of these two-year-olds. Still, word had gotten around that this big bay colt of Sammy Lee's was something special. He was Celebration bound.

Junior liked the feeling that the Hurricane Spray gave him. He had been afraid of it at first. The sound of it scared him, so did the initial cold feel of it. But, he liked what the chemical did. The problem was, it was going to wear off soon.

Sammy rode Junior back to the equipment cart where he had Jeremy nail twenty-ounce lead weights to the pads at the bottom of Junior's front feet. Then the two men put the tail brace on the colt. Even though his tail had been cut and set, it needed the brace to hold it up and make it look right during the class. The brace was uncomfortable to Junior but he accepted it without much fuss. The Hurricane Spray was beginning to wear off and he was much more concerned about that than what they were doing to his tail.

Jeremy placed a pair of four-ounce chains on the colt and helped Sammy get back on. The trainer jerked Junior's head up and took off across the grass. Other horses were warming up and Junior was trying to take in all he could. The strange horses, all these people, new noises and smells, all this was exciting stuff to the young bay stallion.

Sammy Lee's heavy hands and the light, but very painful pair of chains kept his mind on business. The lydocaine was definitely wearing off and the four-ounce chains felt heavier and more painful with each step. After a couple more passes, Junior was ridden back to their spot along the fence. Sammy remained mounted while Jeremy swapped out the chains, trading the fours for a pair of sixes.

Their class was called and Sammy headed Junior toward the show ring. Junior saw Tim Sutton mount his big black colt and spur the horse forward. The colt made a strange move with his front legs. As his left foot came down, he suddenly jerked it back up before it could touch the ground and came down with his right foot. He didn't want to let this foot hit the ground either and with most of his and his rider's weight on his hind legs there was a split-second of awkward confusion, as the colt seemed to not know what to do. His legs tangled and he fell to his knees. Sutton, still in the saddle, spurred and cursed the colt back to his feet. His steps became less tentative as he moved ahead but the poor colt was obviously very, very sore.

Sammy Lee could see that Tim had his hands full. If he could keep his colt under control and keep him from falling down, he would be tough to beat. Sammy knew he had Junior working well but he didn't feel that he had peaked just yet. Apparently, young Sutton had pulled out all the stops to try to beat him tonight.

There were just eight colts in the class. Junior was the fourth one to enter the ring. His entrance brought a cheer from some of the crowd and a few people called out to Sammy. Junior didn't feel so good anymore. The pain in his lower legs was getting worse. His flat walk was slow and painful. Thankfully, Sammy stopped him before they made a complete round of the ring to wait for the rest of the entries to enter the class. It felt good to stand still for a moment.

Tim Sutton and the black were the last to enter the ring, well after the others were in. The announcer had threatened to close the gate and call the class when the big black colt finally came crawling in. The crowd went wild. Some of the more vocal fans started yelling: "Struttin' Sutton, Struttin' Sutton."

Junior could see why. As Sammy spurred him into action, he directed him to the rail opposite the black colt. Junior could see from the corner of his eye how the other horse was squatting and reaching. Tim Sutton was riding hunched over with his feet through the stirrups and his heels in the horse's flanks. His hands were almost to shoulder level and he was bobbing his head along with that of the colt he was riding.

Although there were eight colts in the ring, it was really only a two-horse class. It would be between the very sore Junior and the even more sore black colt of Tim's for first place. Junior could feel the chains biting into his legs in earnest when the announcer asked for the first running walk. Sammy dug in his spurs and Junior responded with more speed and more action. The other colt was doing so much in the flat walk he could barely move on when asked to. There was virtually no difference between his flat walk and his running walk but the crowd still loved what he was doing. Cheers and applause followed him around the ring. Junior had a following, too.

The class was called back to a flat walk and asked to reverse direction. This was a two-year-old "specialty", or two-gait class, and the horses would not be asked to canter. The riders all took this opportunity to rest their mounts a few moments before turning around. Some of them adjusted the curb chain while others just sat there looking at or talking to the crowd.

Junior was grateful for the brief rest. His front feet were killing him. Sammy was really in his mouth tonight. For all its hype and excitement, he was not too thrilled with this horse show thing.

Sammy Lee was restless. He jerked Junior back to the rail in the opposite direction at a flat walk. He gave the colt's head two quick, hard jerks and spurred him roughly as he shifted in the saddle. He took him a bit faster than they had gone the first direction. One by one the other horses took to the rail, with a little prodding by the announcer. The black colt seemed to be hurting even more this way of the ring, if that was possible. Junior did too. The effects of the Hurricane Spray were a distant memory at this point.

When the announcer asked for the running walk this time around, Junior felt a deeper dig of the spurs and a tighter hold on the reins. He gave it all he had. He was reaching and driving with his hind legs and using his shoulders and reaching in front, flipping his front feet out in front of him. Junior was making Sammy, his owners, and the audience very happy.

On the other side of the ring, Tim Sutton was trying to get the black colt to show more speed. He was spurring him with every step but the colt just couldn't move on. He was doing too much. All of a sudden, the Sutton colt got his feet tangled up again and almost went down. The judge was watching Junior at the time and had his back to Tim Sutton. He signaled the announcer to have the horses line up and walked to the end of the ring in front of the grandstand while jotting in his note pad.

As the judge and steward walked down the line of horses and looked them over, Junior tried to catch his breath. His feet hurt, his sides hurt from all the spurring, and it felt as if the bit had rubbed a raw spot on one side of his mouth. Despite the pain, Junior used the opportunity to peruse the crowd. His ears were up and curious. Junior struck a very handsome pose, easily the most handsome of the class.

The black colt, on the other hand, was less optimistic looking. He stood with all four feet so close together that he resembled a circus elephant standing on a platform, preparing to lift one or more of his legs in a trick. Tim Sutton got the horse to park out a little more normally before the judge reached them but he couldn't make him put his ears up or act interested in anything. The colt just stood there in wide-eyed wonder and shock at the intensity of the pain he had just been through, and, in fact, was still feeling.

The crowd was about evenly split between the two favorite horses. Sammy and Tim Sutton both thought they had won the class. Tim was a little more confidant than Sammy, though, for good reason. The judge was a lifelong friend of Tim's father, Bobby, and besides a very friendly phone call the week before, this judge had received a thick envelope of cash supplied by the owners of the black colt. Tim Sutton had no doubt who would win this class.

When his number was called first, Tim and his mount

received almost as many boos as cheers from the divided crowd. Sammy Lee was hot. He knew Junior had won the class. That black colt never even got out of a flat walk. He almost fell down at least once. Sammy had hoped to take Junior to the Celebration without getting beat, high hopes, but not unrealistic. An undefeated run before the big show could mean a lot, create a buzz. Now that was impossible.

Junior and Sammy Lee received a large applause when they picked up the red ribbon for second place. Sammy took the long way out of the ring so he could show the colt off some more. The crowd loved it, although a smattering of boos were heard from the Sutton camp.

"That sumbitch got to the judge, I guarantee it," Sammy told Jeremy back at the trailer. "He won't get away with that again! No sir! I'm gonna make sure Junior wins from here on out. No matter what it costs."

Old Timer tried to console his young friend: "Don't feel bad about not winnin', Junior. That other colt won because he was in even more pain than you were. Besides that, they probably bribed the judge. It's not your fault."

"Yeah, I know. You're right. I need to let it go. Besides, what's really bothering me is the constant pain I'm in and how all the other horses at the show were in similar shape. The stories you tell me about the olden days make me proud to be who I am, part of this wonderful breed with this wonderful heritage. Then I look at what I have to go through on a daily basis, along with the other horses in the barn. I go to a show and see all the sore horses. The so-called 'inspection' is a joke. And, the sorest horse wins! What's going on, Old Timer? Where's the justice? Where's the honor in that? Isn't there something somebody can do, someway to stop this insanity?"

"Junior, I wish I knew the answer. I really wish I knew the

answer to that. What I do know is that the great horses I've been tellin' you about that were responsible for the creation of this here breed of ours would be fightin' mad if they knew it had come to this. That, to be born a Tennessee Walking Horse has become a curse instead of a blessing. I'll bet ya ol' McMeen's Traveler, Hambletonian, the Grey Johns, the Brooks, Stonewall Jackson, the Tom Hals, the Mountain Slashers, Queen, Justin Morgan, all the great horses of the past would jump up and come a fightin' if they knew what was goin' on. I truly believe that. Maybe they'd know what to do, Junior. Maybe they'd know."

"When I saw that black colt I was showing against fall down from being so sore, I really felt sorry for him. I wanted to help him somehow, even though he was my competition."

"I know how you feel, Son. When I see what gets done to you and these other poor horses in this barn I want to help, but I can't. I guess that's one reason I live in the past so much. It gives me strength."

"I know what you mean 'cause those stories you tell, they help me too. I feel a real connection to my ancestors, to their spirit, their nobility. I quit feeling sorry for myself when I think about them, how some of them fought in that bloody, awful war and survived. Even the ones that were killed, their spirit survived, was passed on through blood. I think of the ones after the war who pulled plows, ran races, pulled or carried humans down hundreds of miles of roads, worked on plantations, competed in the first horse shows. I think of how all the right bloodlines came together, seemingly by chance, to come to this. All of those horses lived and reproduced to produce you and me and the black colt that beat me at the show and all the other horses at the show and in this barn."

"Well put, Junior. Well put. We exist because of them. It's hard to believe that such noble spirits and circumstances convened to create this noble breed, just so's we could endure such ignoble treatment."

"Exactly, Old Timer, well put yourself. There's got to be more to it."

"Maybe there is Junior. Maybe there's a way to turn all this around. I hope I live to see it if there is. Maybe the answer is in the past. That's the direction I keep leanin'.

"Remember how I was tellin' you about Old Tom Hal, how he was the sire of Bald Stockings. Well I'm pretty sure I would find him on my family tree somewhere if I went back far enough. Ya see I know I come from a later Tom Hal who must have been descended from the old guy. You follow me?"

"I think so."

"Well, Junior, it's through my grandsire, Midnight Sun. His mother's father's mother was a daughter of Brown Hal, Jr., got that? Brown Hal was a son of Gibson's Tom Hal and a brother to the very famous Little Brown Jug. Along with their other brother, Hal Pointer, these were the three fastest pacers to come from any one sire, ever. So, Brown Hal Jr. was a registered Standardbred and his mama was a Morgan mare, goin' back to Black Hawk through Black Hawk's Rattler. You put all this together with the bloodlines of one of the greatest all-time Walking Horse sires, Wilson's Allen, and you get my granddaddy, Midnight Sun. He won the World Grand Championship in 1945 and 1946 and went on to produce more champions than anybody."

"How do you remember all that stuff Old Timer?"

"Sometimes I wonder that myself Junior. Sometimes I wonder that myself. I guess it's partly because, like I said, at my age I live mostly in the past anyway. Got nothin' better to do.

"Now, if you look at the other side of my granddaddy's family, the Wilson's Allen side, you're lookin' at some absolute royalty there too, Junior, if I do say so myself. Wilson's Allen's sire was the great Roan Allen who, of course, was by ol' Black Allan. His dam was Birdie Messick who was also by Allan. Five of the first six horses to be named Grand Champion Walking Horse of the World were by Wilson's Allen."

"That's pretty impressive."

"Your darn right, that's impressive. Even more impressive, they say, was his daddy, ol' Roan Allen. He was, let's see now, my great, great, grandsire, Junior. It's been told that Roan Allen was so smart and talented he could do seven different show gaits, seven of 'em, and perform them impeccably. He would show in plantation classes, combination classes, where they worked him to cart and under saddle, and five-gaited classes, almost always winnin'. He even beat Roe's Chief a couple times in gaited classes. And Roe's Chief was a Saddlebred. I heard that one of the men that used to show Roan Allen a lot used to enter the ring with a glass of water in his hand. He would carry that glass all the way around the ring just to show how smooth the old horse was. This always made quite an impression, of course, and probably helped him win a few classes. Ain't nothin' wrong with a little showmanship, Junior. No sir.

"Another great sire of Wilson's Allen's time was Merry Boy, and he was also a double-grandson of ol' Allan. He lived to be thirty-two years old and got mares in foal at thirty-one. Merry Boy's mama was one of the greatest show mares who ever lived and at the same time one of the most important broodmares of our breed. She hardly ever got beat in the show ring and was often shown soon after weaning a colt. Sometimes she showed and won while her foal was a waitin' in a stall, back at the barn. I'm talkin' about the great Merry Legs, Junior.

"Most of the time when I'm talkin' about our history like this it's easy to mention mostly the stallions simply because they physically have more offspring. You and I both know the mares are just as important. To us they were more important because they raised us. In the overall scheme of things there are a few great mares that really stand out and Merry Legs was one of them.

Later on there was Black Angel, a great show mare, who I share a special bond with. She wasn't known so much for her offspring like Merry Legs was, but, in her day, she was hardly ever beat in the show ring. She was one of the few mares to win the World Grand Championship."

"I didn't know a mare ever won the big stake, Old Timer."

"Well, they don't anymore, haven't in years. Guess it wouldn't be economical."

"What do you mean?"

"Well, I mean it's a lot more profitable for a stallion to win the big prize so's his owners can demand the big breedin' fees, breed hundreds of mares, and make lots of money. Can't do that with a mare or gelding, now can they?"

"No, I guess not. I see your point Old Timer. And, it's true mostly you hear about the great stallions of the ages more than the mares. I guess I understand why, the way you explained it, but it still doesn't seem hardly fair. Of course, nothing much in this world seems fair to me right now."

SIX

Early in the West Coast show season Royal Riggins Stables traveled to the Earl Warren Showgrounds in Santa Barbara, California. Roy believed this was one of the most attractive showgrounds in the country. He wasn't the only one to think so, either. Nestled in the foothills at the edge of the beautiful seaside town, it was always a pleasure to come here for a week or so and show horses. Roy usually came here for the "Channel City" show and again in July, right after the San Diego County Fair in Del Mar.

Socks liked it right away. It was the air he liked, right off the ocean. He had never been this close to the ocean before, hadn't even known what to expect. The trailer window was partially open on the way up from Chino. When they hit the coast highway, Socks could smell the sea. The water, the salt, the fish, the seaweed entered his nostrils like a breath of spring. He didn't know exactly what it all was but he liked it just the same. When he was unloaded at their assigned barn, he was feeling so good he just had to jump around a little bit, even though he was tired from the trip. He was young and this was all new to him. Normally mild mannered Socks raised his tail in the air, snorted twice, and hit three bounding steps of a straight trot on the way to his stall.

His stall was bedded in fresh straw instead of shavings. Of course, Socks had to eat some of it and lie down and try to roll. When he got up he saw that he was next to Lacey, with the tack room on the other side.

"Now don't eat too much of that straw young sir, or you will be sorry. We'll all be fed soon enough." Lacey scolded.

"Yes, Miss Lacey, I hear ya. I'm just kinda playing around. I feel so good up here."

"It is nice isn't it? The ocean air, I mean."

"Oh, I'll say! When do we eat?" Socks just couldn't contain his enthusiasm.

"I don't know for sure, but I'd say it won't be long. They've got a lot of unloading and setting up to do. These people will treat you right. You know that. You'll get fed at regular hours. Your stall will be cleaned twice a day, more if you need it."

"I expect nothing less! Just kidding, Miss Lacey."

"Like I said before, you ought to be grateful for what you've got, for how well you are treated, young sir! Let me tell you something. We were stabled behind some Walking Horses at The Los Angeles Forum last year that didn't get fed until noon. Their water buckets weren't attached, so they knocked them over in the night and never had anything to drink. They didn't even have enough bedding to cover the floor of the stall and at The Forum that means asphalt. On top of that, they were sore as could be. So count your blessings, Socks."

"Oh I do Miss Lacey, I do. I guess all California trainers aren't like Royal Riggins, is that what you're sayin'?"

"I don't think there are many like him anywhere, especially in the Walking Horse business. And I'm not the only one who thinks so. Royal Riggins actually has some rather famous fans, Socks.

"Why just a few years back up at the Cow Palace in San Francisco, the Governor of California presented Roy with the championship trophy. My friend, April Love, was the horse he was riding. She and Roy never got beat as far as I know. Anyway, the Cow Palace has always been a big show, Socks. They alternate horse show classes with rodeo events and have the National Finals there so the crowds are large and loud. I guess that's why the governor was there. It's a big deal for the state. Anyway, the governor's name was Ronald Reagan and he recognized Roy right off. When he presented Roy with the trophy he told him what a good job he'd done, and he said:

"'I thought I recognized you from somewhere, Roy, recognized the way you sit a horse. Then, well, when they called your name, I remembered. You used to ride the Rancheros trail ride with us every year. You and your friends always had some mighty fine horses. Well, congratulations, Roy, and best of luck. You're one heck of a horseman.'"

"I'm impressed," said Socks.

"One afternoon up at that same Cow Palace show, Roy got to the barn to find Roy Rogers and Dale Evans sitting on one of his tack trunks eating fried chicken. They were sitting right next to my stall so I heard Roy Rogers tell Roy Riggins that they sure enjoyed watching him show the night before. He said:

"'That pretty bay mare you were riding just looked so natural compared to a lot of the Walking Horses we've been seeing lately.' Then, Missus Dale told him:

"'She was a real joy to watch, Roy, a real joy.' Of course, they were talking about yours truly, Socks. Our Roy said his thank you's and not much else. I think he mumbled something about enjoying their act. They were the special event that year. He seemed to be just a little taken aback to find these two sitting on his tack trunk in the middle of the afternoon. I guess Mr. Rogers caught that, too, so he explained:

"'I don't know if you know it or not Roy, but Big Jim used to work for me and Dale years ago. When we saw him go in the ring last night to carry your trophy for you we thought we better look him up and see if his fried chicken is as good as it used to be. Let me tell you, I think it may have gotten better.'

"Then Missus Dale said: 'I would just like to say again what a joy it is to watch your horses show. Especially with all the terrible things we have heard about and seen happening to Walking Horses lately. You know our Triggers are registered Tennessee Walking Horses and we just love this breed, but hate what's going on.'

"Royal Riggins said: 'I figured Trigger was a Walking Horse. Of course, I knew Gene Autry's horse, Champion, was because I was there in Tennessee when he bought him from S. W. Beech. I guess they bought him mostly for his looks. I'll never forget how Mr. Autry's trainer thought the horse had a little too much walk but he would get that out of him as soon as they got home.'

"Well, that put a big grin on Roy Rogers' face, Socks, and he said: 'I remember Gene telling me Champ leaned toward the trotty side so they'd get him to trot, or do a slow flat walk, or gallop most of the time when they were shooting. Still, the horse would slip into a nice little four-beat running walk now and then and Gene would try to keep him in it. The director would get mad and yell cut then Gene would start singing, "I'm just trying to make it easier on my poor ol' posterior." He made a little song out of it. He really got a kick out of that and he loves those horses of his. Just like we do.'"

"A lot of famous horses were Tennessee Walking Horses weren't they Miss Lacey?"

"Yes, I suppose so, quite a few."

"Come on now, Socks, let me rub some of that sleep out of your eye. I'm not going to hurt you."

Ricky Riggins was getting Socks ready in his stall. It was

5:00 a.m. The horse's halter was snapped to the crossties they'd put up the night before. His tail set and blanket lay on the tailboard. When Socks was ready, Rick led him up to the warm-up area. These two large, outside paddocks beside the main arena were sometimes used to hold classes. There were just a few other horses being worked at this hour, a jumping horse and two quarter horses. Socks was amazed at the size of the jumping horse and the ease with which she took the practice jumps that were placed around the paddock. He saw one of the quarter horses turn around fast, several times, in one spot. He was literally spinning around on his hind feet. He stopped, set his feet. Then, went a couple rounds in the other direction.

While his son Ricky strapped a pair of lightly weighted, protective leather bell-boots on Socks' front feet, Royal Riggins adjusted the bridle and asked Socks if he thought he could learn to spin like that stock horse over there. Socks didn't answer, but he thought to himself, "There's no way I could do that."

Roy stepped in the saddle and took Socks along the rail at a fast flat walk. Socks shied at a couple of the jumps and there was a wooden bridge the trail horses used to practice with that also got his attention. His trainer calmed him down some and straightened him out. With Roy's help, Socks channeled his excitement into more leg motion. After just once around the large paddock he slowed Socks down and walked him over to the spinning horse and the man in the starched shirt and cowboy hat.

The quarter horse was smaller than Socks. He was a pretty sorrel with a blaze and four white socks.

"That's a pretty colt you've got there, Mack. Is he by that good stud of yours?"

"Yes he is, Roy, as a matter of fact. Kinda favors him, don't he."

"Yeah, he does. Did you bring a bunch up this year?"

"Not too many. I'm trying to cut back some. Ain't getting any younger, you know."

"Oh, I know. Breakfast at Denny's?"

"Sure, sounds good. Come by the barn when you're ready."

Roy walked Socks through an opening in the paddock fence toward the main arena. The horse show arena in Santa Barbara is semi-enclosed. When it rains, the horses and exhibitors get wet, but not the people in the stands. The rail is high, with the first row of box seats actually sitting above the horses. There are two gates at one end of the arena with the announcer's booth in between them. Roy stopped Socks for a moment in the passageway leading to the open gate. He watched as a large chestnut Saddlebred went racing by at a rack. Then Roy urged him into the arena following the big chestnut at a fast flat walk.

It took Socks a while to settle in against the rail. He kept looking up into the stands. There were no people there, but he was just fascinated by the whole place. He'd never seen anything like it. That's one reason his trainer had gotten him up early, so they could get in here before the morning classes started and while it was still dark. Socks was still green and needed to be exposed to things before the limit class on Thursday night.

Roy asked Socks for more speed until he had him doing a good running walk. The colt was getting used to his surroundings and working well against the rail, so he didn't over do it. He slowed him down and asked for a canter. Socks had developed a real nice, "rocking-chair" canter over the past few months. Before making one complete round of the ring Socks was brought back down to a fast flat walk and guided across to the opposite rail at a diagonal, changing directions. Roy took him right on into a running walk, guiding Socks away from the rail at one point to give right of way to the Saddlebred, who was still working the first direction. After cantering on this lead and a little more flat walking, he brought Socks into the center of the arena and parked him close to where Rick was standing.

"He looks good, Dad."

"Feels like he gets better all the time. I think he's ready, don't you?"

"Yep."

As Roy finished the last of his short-stack and coffee he confided in his friend Mack McLain:

"Mack, this sore horse problem keeps getting worse. There for a while I thought we might stop it, but it's getting bigger. It has completely taken over back east, been that way for years now. I couldn't take my best horse back there and expect to get in the money. The guys judging the shows are sore horse trainers. They're not going to tie a clean horse. The sorest horse wins. The only thing that's saving us out here is that most of our classes, at these big shows anyway, are judged by Saddlebred trainers and most of them still appreciate a good, clean, sound going horse."

"What about the inspections? Don't they keep the lame ones out?"

"Out here they do, most the time. Dr. Will has done a great job. We would be a lot worse off if it weren't for him. But, he's feeling pressure now too. He's being challenged more and more. These yahoos come up to him and say, 'Well, how do you know that horse is sore. He ain't sore, he just walks that way, natural.'"

"Of course, you and I know that Dr. Will is one of the top veterinarians in the state, if not the whole country, and it doesn't take a genius to know when a horse is hurting. A horse is either sound or unsound, and you shouldn't be allowed to show an unsound horse."

"It's against American Horse Show rules."

"Right, and in any other breed it wouldn't help you anyway. It would be a hindrance. You try to show a sore Saddlebred for instance. How you going to get him to do a decent trot if his front feet are hurting like that?"

"You've got a point there, Roy. But you know every breed has its share of problems. Nobody's perfect. We have both seen jumping horse guys or gals pole their horses as they go over a jump. I've even seen poles with nails sticking out of them that drew blood. I've seen stock horse trainers run a horse into a fence or a wall to get him to stop. And you know some of your Saddlebred buddies would practically road founder a horse to get him to rack if they had too. It's a competitive game and some times people cross the line. Why, if they were to bust every Western trainer that had ace promizine in his trunk, we'd all be in trouble. Look how hard they push racehorses, of any breed. It's survival of the fittest, and a lot of horses break down along the way, an awful lot."

"Yeah, what you're saying is true, Mack. It's competition, and competition breeds excess. But most of what you're talking about are isolated instances, or training methods used a couple times, then that's it. They're not needed anymore. That doesn't make them right. Don't get me wrong. That's not what I'm saying. It's just that these Walking Horse guys have taken things to a whole different level. It tears me up to see what's happening to this breed. These horses have been my life for a long time now and I just hate the direction things are going. Maybe I'll start showing stock horses. You know, I've got this little Walking colt that's a heck of a cow horse."

"Oh yeah? Now, I'd like to see that."

Socks did great on Thursday night. He was a little frightened of the lights and the crowd but Roy kept him under control and collected. He was the crowd favorite and won the class with a fair amount of ease. His blue ribbon was added to the other blues and reds won by Royal Riggins Stables horses that week that hung outside the show tack room. They won every class in the Walking Horse division at the Santa Barbara show. The red ribbons were from when they had more than one horse entered in the same class. Lacey won the mares and the ladies classes, as usual, and Socks was quite impressed by the whole operation.

Later in the year, toward the end of June, they went to Del Mar, California for the big multi-breed show that was part of the San Diego County Fair. Once again, Socks was treated to a dose of that cool, refreshing, ocean air that he loved. The Chino hills were hot, dry, and smoggy this time of year, and the change was welcome. Socks thought the old adobe barns smelled sort of musty and dusty, and looked like they were a hundred years old. But he got a real treat when, the morning after their arrival, Royal took him out on the racetrack to work.

A low, cool mist still hung over the track though it was beginning to break up and give way to the warm summer sun. As the fog cleared, Socks got a sense of the size of the track. It was huge. Roy rode him to the right, toward the ocean and the back turn. He started out in a fast flat walk then on to a running walk. Socks was going all out as he started to round the turn and saw the huge grandstand looming in front of him. Roy slowed him down and brought the colt to a halt before reaching the homestretch. That was just fine with Socks, as he was apprehensive about making a pass in front of the awesome grandstand. He was, to be honest, just a little bit frightened of the massive structure. So, when Royal turned Socks around and headed back toward the backside, where they had entered the track, the horse felt a sense of relief. As they turned around, Socks caught sight of the Ferris Wheel and The Hammer rides of the fair. He hadn't noticed them on the way out and Roy let him stop and look at them for a moment. The morning sun was glancing off the metal contraptions in a way that fascinated the young horse. Socks loved it when Roy let him take in the scenery like this. His reverie didn't last long, however. There was work to be done.

There weren't many horses out on the track at this time of morning. Most of the racehorses had finished with their workouts, and few show horse people ventured on to the track. Royal picked out a vacant area of the backstretch and cantered Socks in a circle on both leads before taking him back to the barn. He was pleased with the way the colt was working. Socks was really coming into his own.

Roy remained mounted as they left the track but let Socks walk slowly back to the barn, giving him a chance to catch his breath and cool out a bit. Socks had broken a sweat and was just a little winded from his work out. As they walked down the dirt road back to the barn, they were joined by Royal's aging Dalmatian, Midnight. The old dog wagged his tail at the sound of his master's voice and took up along side them at a still springy little trot. Midnight had taken a liking to Socks. The dog sensed the presence of an old soul in the body of the young gelding and they had hit it off right away. Besides, Midnight was named after Socks' grandsire, Midnight Sun. Socks was always happy to have his company. Even though the canine could be cantankerous at times, you couldn't help but love him.

"I don't see how those racehorses run around that whole track, Midnight. It's enormous. I know I couldn't do it, not in a million years," Socks told his friend.

"Of course you couldn't do it in a million years 'cause then, you'd be even older than I am, you silly equine."

"Oh, you always have to act smart, don't you?"

"Well, I am smart. I'm a dog."

"Yeah, you're a dog named after a horse. That makes you alright, I guess, but probably a bit confused."

"Oh, go chew your feed bucket-hey, what the…" Midnight let out a low growl at almost the same moment Socks felt Roy cue him to stop. Their attention was turned to what was taking place between the two barns to their left. A horse had just been unloaded and was being led to his stall. He was being dragged and whipped, would be a more accurate description. The poor horse was really sore. Socks hadn't seen anything like it since leaving Tennessee.

After the small gray gelding was commandeered into his stall, the older of the men, a tall, slightly stooped, dark-haired man wearing a straw fedora and huge sideburns, yelled out in an overly friendly manner:

"Hey, Roy, how you doing? Haven't seen you in a while. See you still got that old spotted dog tagging along."

"I'm not too old to tear you apart in about two minutes, you old piece of southern fried chicken," Socks heard the dog mutter under his breath.

"Yeah, still got him, or he's got me, not sure which it is," Roy said, amicably enough. "And you're still up to your old tricks I see, Mr. Rust," he told himself as he patted Socks on the neck and continued towards their barn.

"Boy, I hate to see that."

"Who was that?" Socks asked Midnight, who still had a corner of his lip curled in disgust.

"That was one Leonard Rust, a disgusting human being who calls himself a horse trainer. He's as bad as they come, Socks, as bad as they come."

SEVEN

The junior class, a class for Tennessee Walking Horses four years old and under, was to be held on Wednesday the Fourth of July at Del Mar this year. It would be Socks' first junior class, and his first time showing on the Fourth at the big fair. There would be plenty of fireworks.

The morning of the Fourth, Midnight slipped in to talk to Socks while Ricky was cleaning his stall. He said:

"I think today's the day, Socks, I can feel it in my old aching bones. Later on tonight, the sky will light up and you'll hear the most dreadful, deafening sounds. They'll have to lock me in the tack room or I'll run away. It sounds like a war zone around here on the Fourth of July and I admit I get scared out of my spots."

"Oh, I've heard firecrackers before and they're not so bad. I think you're probably exaggerating, Still Spotted One."

"Hey, the name is Midnight remember? And this is a lot more than firecrackers I'm talking about, although I don't think much of them either. I guess dogs are more sensitive to this sort of thing. But I'm not just whistling Yankee Doodle Dandy. I'm warning you. I can feel it. Something's going to happen tonight and it's not gonna be good."

"Well, thanks for the warning but I'm sure I can handle it," Socks tried to sound brave.

Young Rick finished shaking out the stall and he and Midnight moved on down the row. Socks stuck his head out over the stall door to see what was going on. Lacey had her head out already, waiting to feel the warmth of the morning sun. As the fog lifted and shifted and the sunlight grew brighter, the edge of it moved towards her stall. Soon after it was released from the shadow of the barn to their east, the wonderful, warm light was caught up by the overhang of her own roof. But for a few precious moments, if she hung her head in just the right spot, she was basked in its warmth. When shadow once again covered her face she realized that Socks was talking to her.

"I'm sorry, what were you saying?"

"I was telling you Midnight said a lot of bad stuff is gonna happen tonight."

"Oh, he's just getting jittery because he knows it's the Fourth of July. That old canine is awfully smart, downright perceptive at times, but he's most likely just overreacting because of the day. As brave and wise as he is, these fireworks turn him into a whimpering little pup. I'm not thrilled about them myself, but I do have some self-control and have gotten somewhat used to the situation. Poor old Midnight acts the same now as when we first came down here years ago. And he's been coming here a lot longer than I have. He knows what's coming. I guess he'll never get used to it."

"May be, but the way he was talkin' Miss Lacey, he seemed concerned about more than just the fireworks though, like something else was gonna happen, something bad."

"Like I said, he is very smart. And he does feel things coming sometimes."

"Great, my class is tonight and I heard Roy tellin' Ricky that little gray horse we saw Leonard Rust unloading is his hot new four-year old, straight from Tennessee. Rust has a new assistant trainer, a young car mechanic who is really into the chemicals. The two of them came down here with just two horses. They've been bragging on how they're gonna show everybody 'how it's done'."

"Now Socks, don't worry yourself too much. As bad as they are, those guys can't hurt you. I feel sorry for those horses of theirs, though, even if they are the competition."

"Roy said they must know something about this judge or they wouldn't be here."

"Well, that may be. They might think he will tie their sored up horses but they've got to get them into the class first, and Dr. Will has been doing a pretty good job of keeping the real sore ones out lately. Don't worry about things you can't control."

That evening, with Midnight securely locked in the tack room, Socks and Ricky and Royal Riggins headed to the inspection area. Socks was shining from head to toe. His hooves were painted. His mane and tail shimmered in the artificial light as the sun went down. Even his eyes shone. He was excited but even-tempered, cool. His tail brace was on but not yet fastened underneath. His black bridle had a black, patent leather brow band with white diamonds lined across it that set off the white on his face and matched the black and white ribbon that had been braided into his mane and forelock. He was looking sharp and feeling sharp. But in the back of his mind, the words of that darn dog he loved so much kept haunting him. Was something bad going to happen tonight? Could a dog really have such premonitions, a sixth sense? Hadn't he had such feelings himself in the past? His mother had certainly told him of more than one occasion when her senses had warned her of danger. She had said that certain horses were better at this than others. She had even told him as a youngster that she thought he had some kind of gift.

Well, how come he didn't sense anything now? She had told him it was the sort of thing you got better at with age. Probably he just wasn't old enough to know all these things. Or, more probably, Midnight was feeling more arthritis in his old bones than anything else.

As they neared the inspection area, Socks could tell something was wrong without any mysterious sixth sense. He could hear men arguing. Leonard Rust was cussing and yelling, pointing his finger at Dr. Will, getting in his face. The veterinarian was standing his ground, pointing at the gray colt they had brought up to inspection. The colt was just as sore as when Socks had first seen him.

"Now, Mr. Rust that's where you're wrong, I do have the authority. That's my job as official veterinarian of this horse show. Your horse is sore. He's lame, and under American Horse Show Rules, I cannot allow you to compete."

"I'm telling you he ain't sore! And you can't prove it! Just let us in and we'll let the judge decide."

"I must ask you to step aside and let the next entry up for inspection." Insisted Dr. Will.

"What seems to be the problem, Will?" said Royal Riggins as he led Socks forward.

"Oh, Mr. Rust here just has a problem accepting reality, accepting the consequences of his actions."

"Now see here. This has nothing to do with you, Riggins. This is between me and the doc."

"So you're saying that colt isn't sore, is that it?" Roy knew he was butting in but he couldn't help it.

"Like I said, this has nothing to do with you. The doc says he's sore. I say he's not. Sort of a stand off the way I see it. I say I have a right to show my horse, as much right as anybody! The entry fee's been paid."

"All the entry fees in the world don't give you the right to treat a horse like that. Why, he can barely stand up." Roy's temper was rising fast, Socks could sense it and it was making him nervous.

"I told you for the last time, butt out, Riggins!" Leonard Rust handed the reins of the gray colt to his assistant, the young car mechanic from Tennessee. He moved to the side of the colt and seemed to be adjusting something on the saddle when he suddenly stepped toward Socks and Royal. In his right hand was a riding crop, raised and swinging for Roy's head. Socks jumped back as Roy threw his reins to Ricky. Then Roy feinted to his right and ducked under the swipe of the whip. As Rust finished his swing, Roy finished him with a left to the jaw. Laid him flat. Socks saw a glint of steel in the car mechanic's right hand. He was the only one to see the threatening blade that night. At that moment, two San Diego County Sheriff's deputies arrived with Dr. Bill Tulles of the Humane Society. Socks thought he saw the car mechanic turned horse trainer throw something into the bushes.

As the deputies picked Leonard Rust up off the ground, Bill Tulles took the reins of the gray colt from his assistant trainer and said: "I'm impounding this animal and placing the two of you under arrest for cruelty to animals. You have the right to remain silent..."

"You're arresting us? What about this son of a bitch that just hit me? You ought to be arresting him for assault."

"I'm sorry Mr. Rust, it looked more like self-defense to me. Didn't you think so, Deputies?"

"I thought so," One of them said.

"Of course, we could always add assault to the counts against you if Mr. Riggins here would care to press charges."

"Oh, I'm alright Bill, just a little misunderstanding." Roy took Socks' reins from his son and rubbed the horse on the neck. "If you need any witnesses as to what those two have done to that poor colt, I'm at your disposal."

Roy could feel Leonard's stare burning into the side of his

face. He turned and met the man's gaze as the sheriff's deputies took him away.

"I think that's about enough excitement for this evening. Don't you Socks, old boy? How'd you manage that, Will?"

"Well, Dr. Tulles called me and said he'd like to sit in on a few inspections again this year. I'm always glad to have the support, especially these days. We could see these yahoos coming a mile away. When Bill saw how badly that poor colt was walking, how much pain he was in, he lost it. He told me he had to do something. He said: 'This is what the Humane Society is all about, trying to stop this kind of nonsense.' Then he said: 'Hold down the fort, Will, I'll be right back.' That's when he went to get the sheriff's deputies."

Dr. Will picked up Socks' right front and was inspecting him as he talked.

"It's getting worse all the time, Roy. I feel like we're manning the last bastion, trying to hold out against the odds. These guys get braver and more blatant at each show. Maybe Dr. Bill can make an example of those two, and show some of the others, that there are serious consequences for this kind of thing."

"I hope so but I think you're right; we are fighting the odds. The sore horse people have been in control so long back east that a lot of the new guys and gals coming up don't even know that there's any other way of training these horses. Look at that guy Rust has with him, what's his name, Sammy Belford? I heard he was a car mechanic until a couple years ago. Heard he married some money, had a horse in training with Rust, then got the training bug. I guess he figured if he could make an engine run he could train a horse to walk. Makes sense to me."

"Did you mean it when you told Bill Tulles that you would testify."

"You bet, Will. I'll be there if I'm needed. You can count on it."

"Thanks, Roy, I appreciate it. Would you lead this colt out

there for me? Turn him to the right, real tight. That's it, now to the left. All right, that's good. You better get on and get warmed up if you need to. You're the last one through and they're about to call your class."

Just as Roy swung his leg up over Sock's back, the fireworks started. Socks leaped forward as his rider gathered the reins. Roy brought the colt under control while reaching for his off side stirrup. Socks had calmed down after the Leonard Rust incident but the sudden whistling followed by the explosion of light and noise of the pyrotechnics took him by surprise. However, as Midnight had surmised, Socks was an old soul and he trusted the man on his back. He believed in this man who had ridden his sire and even his grandsire once upon a time. This man who stood for the old way of training without gimmicks, without chemicals, who was willing to stand up to the bad guys, to fight for what is right.

Socks entered the ring with a huge surge of adrenalin, yet totally under the control of his rider. Royal Riggins had his own surge of adrenalin pumping and the pair of them put on a performance that became the talk of the show. The other colts in the class didn't have a chance. Mack McLain came up to Roy after the class and asked him if that was the same colt he'd had up at Santa Barbara. Roy said;

"He's the same one, alright."

"Well, he sure looked different. Everybody's talking about him, about the show you just made."

"Yeah, he felt real good tonight, kind of came into his own, I think. Maybe the fireworks helped him along a little."

"Speaking of fireworks, I heard you had a little fireworks yourself, before the class. Heard they arrested two Walking Horse trainers. Is it true that you knocked one of 'em out, Roy?"

"I probably shouldn't have. But he was sure asking for it, took a swing at me with a whip. I just hope I don't have to pay for it later, somehow."

"What do you mean? You're not afraid of them are you?"

"No, I'm not afraid of guys like them. I just don't trust them. They're the kind that like to get even. They're snakes. And I know they have no qualms about hurting animals. Like I said, I just don't trust them."

"Well, watch your back, my friend. If there's ever anything I can do, you just let me know, you hear."

"Alright, thanks Mack."

After Socks was cooled out and put up for the night, Lacey listened to him recount the evening's events.

"You know Miss Lacey, old Midnight kept sayin' how something bad was gonna happen tonight, but it wasn't so bad. Everything turned out all right."

"You're still feeling uppity after winning your class, Socks. The fact is, something bad did happen. That might not be the end of it, either."

"I have a right to feel uppity from what everybody says."

"Yes, you do. I'm not saying you don't. I'm just saying that what happened before the class with those two characters from Tennessee is not good, not good at all."

"Well, they caught 'em. They hauled them off to jail. That's good ain't it?"

"Yes, well… we'll see."

As Socks nibbled on some hay in the corner he tried to digest what it was that Lacey meant, exactly. A few nights later he placed second in the gentleman's class to a horse called Bandolero ridden by Bob Fields. Socks worked well in the class. He just didn't have the magic he'd displayed on the Fourth of July.

Midnight tried to console him. "It's alright Socks. Everybody has a bad day. Everybody has especially good days, too. That night of the Fourth, I didn't see it of course, 'cause I was hiding under the cot in the tack room, everybody says you were fantastic. They're still talking about it. The stars were aligned for you that night, my friend. You came into your own. You were a star. You still are but that was a special night and you have to realize that. The thing to remember is, as Roy says, 'if you can do it once you can learn to do it all the time.'"

"I don't know. I hope so."

Lacey won the mares, ladies, and amateur classes, making her high-point Walking Horse of the show. Her owners took home a big trophy and Socks was extremely proud of her. After Del Mar, the stable traveled up the coast to Santa Barbara again where they won every class in their division. The rest of the show season they continued to win. More often than not, Roy Riggins' horses came out on top. Socks won a few junior classes, a gentleman's class, and even got second to Lacey in a ladies class once with Mack McLain's wife, Karin, riding. That was the highlight of the year for Socks. He never let the poor mare forget how he "almost beat" her.

The next couple years went pretty much the same with Royal Riggins Stables being the dominant Walking Horse string. Socks did his share of winning, developing into a fine show horse. He didn't win all the time, though. Bob Fields had a horse that beat him more than once. The Mussleman family had some good horses that occasionally took the blue from Royal Riggins and his bunch. Frank Littrell got hold of a real nice black mare that gave Lacey a run for her money. Overall, through most of the 70's, as in the 60's and 50's, it was the Royal treatment that prevailed.

Royal Riggins was subpoenaed to testify in the animal cruelty trial against Leonard Rust and Sammy Lee Belford. He did so willingly and honestly, hoping the court would make an example of the two and help turn the tide against the sore-horse mentality. The judge sentenced Rust to probation and prohibited him from showing for ten years in the state of California. Belford got simple probation, as it was harder to prove him directly culpable, and he continued to show on the West Coast. It was at the Indio Date Festival that he sought to get his revenge and earned the nickname of Sammy the Snake.

The 1970's brought about more changes in the Walking Horse industry. The Horse Protection Act, passed at the beginning of the decade, included a scar rule that was getting increasingly difficult for the chemically-dependant trainers to comply with. Straight oil of mustard just left too many scars. They had to find other, less visible ways of soring these horses. It has been said that fear of prosecution is the mother of invention, or something like that.

During the 1970's and since, Walking Horses have been found with nails in their quick, golf balls in their frog, and other inventive methods designed to train through pain. Golf balls cut in half and placed between the bottom of the horse's hoof and the leather or plastic pads put pressure on the tender frog area in the sole of the foot with every step. No outwardly visible scarring results. Some people even put pieces of high-tension spring and ball bearings in this tender area. Often rocks or stones are used, and then the trainer claims innocence if caught, saying that's not a "foreign" or illegal substance. "It must have just worked its way in there somehow." Horses' front hooves got shorter and shorter over the years, while the stack of pads and the size of the shoes got larger and larger. Many Walking Horse farriers became experts at trimming the hoof down to the quick, the living tissue, as close as possible without drawing blood, but close enough to cause a lot of pain when the animal put his weight on it.

The stories are endless and monstrous, unbelievable, yet true. Socks heard about some frightening goings on from Lacey and Midnight and other horses at the shows. He wondered why people thought they had to do these things to their horses, to his relatives. Don't they realize what a great breed this is, that it isn't necessary to hurt these horses to make them prettier, or make their gait more attractive? The opposite in fact is true.

Then the real shocker came. Tennessee Walking Horses were

no longer to be shown with the protective leather bell-boots strapped below their front ankles. They were to be shown with chains and, in the interim, weighted leather bands, or collars, could be used.

"In the show ring, Midnight, are you sure? Chains?" Socks exclaimed.

"Sure as I'm standing here. It's already happening. I heard Roy talking about it last night. They call the leather bands 'dog collars' of all things. I wish they wouldn't get dogs involved in all this."

"Yeah, but chains? That's ridiculous. It's embarrassing. No other breed of horse shows with chains on. A lot of special gaited horses are trained at home with chains and rattlers and such, like we are, but not in the show ring. Who's bright idea was that?"

"Roy says there must be some reason behind it. He says they've found some new chemicals that don't blister as much or cause scars like straight oil of mustard. He says they have a way of making the skin hypersensitive but it works best with chains. They can make a little six-ounce chain feel like twenty-ounces with spikes coming out of it. They can draw these new chemicals into the skin with DMSO, whatever that is, and plastic wrap. He says that chains work a lot better with these new methods, that bell-boots don't have enough of a bite. It's the combination of these chemicals with chains that works the best, or hurts the most, however you look at it. They got the rules changed to fit their methods."

"The USDA is going along with all this? The government is going to let this happen?" Socks couldn't believe what he was hearing.

Midnight continued: "Oh yeah, these people have manipulated the government into playing right into their hands. That's how powerful they have become. The USDA has even sanctioned a new kind of inspector called a DQP, a Designated Qualified Person, to take over the inspection process at the shows."

"'A Designated Qualified Person?' Sounds like a bunch of designated qualified dog poop to me. What does a 'DQP' know about a horse, whether he is sound or not? What does one of them know that a good vet like Dr. Will doesn't know?"

"Nothing, except where their money comes from," it was Lacey speaking up for the first time.

"What do you mean, Miss Lacey? What do you know about all this?" Socks asked.

"I heard some people talking about it. Apparently these new inspectors are going to be chosen and trained and paid, in part, by the industry people."

"So, the same bunch of humans that are coming up with all these new ways to sore horses are gonna have the inspectors in their back pockets? Man, what could be worse?" asked Socks.

"Not much, according to Roy," said Midnight. "For the first time in my life I heard him talking about quitting this business. Just the other night he was sitting in that old chair of his when he reached down and scratched me behind the ear and told me he didn't know if he could take it much longer."

"But if he quits, what will we do? Who will train us?" Socks wondered.

"There are still a few clean trainers left," said Lacey.

"Yeah, but how many, two? Three? And none as good as Roy Riggins."

"Maybe Ricky will carry the torch, keep it in the family."

"Could be, but I think he's just as disillusioned as his father. Besides, he wants to be a singing star. 'Bright lights, big city,' and all that."

EIGHT

Junior's defeat at such an early and small show was really eating at Sammy Lee. He couldn't let that happen again. Junior was his big shot this year, one of his best chances to win at the Celebration, the World Championship contest. The next time he showed the colt he would make sure he'd be doing something freaky so that no one could beat him, not even that conniving little sneak, Tim Sutton. Junior's training intensified, not so much as in hours in the saddle, but in the amount of pain he had to endure. Sammy and Jeremy began injecting some of the caustic chemicals directly under the skin of Junior's forelegs. As his training and pain intensified, so did his dreams.

These dreams most often took him to the surreal, quasi-Civil War setting inhabited by versions of Sammy and William and Jeremy who captured and tortured him. Just as often as the men sored him, mystical horses showed up to rescue him. There was the sorrel Traveler, the gray they called John, and a beautiful strong bay horse known as Chief, among others. Chief was the horse that Junior felt closest to for some reason. He was more like himself in size and confirmation, a more modern looking horse. Junior began to recognize Traveler, who was one of the leaders, as McMeen's Traveler, the great sire of war-horses that Old Timer had told him about. He knew that the gray, John, must be Boone's Gray John. Several of the other horses that joined him in his dreams he recognized as historic figures from Old Timer's stories. There was the unmistakable Bald Stockings, Earnhart's Brooks, the great war-horse King Phillip. He thought he recognized, though he wasn't sure how, the mares Merry Legs, and Black Angel; Roan Allen; and even ol' Allan himself. Sometimes there were more horses than he could count, but most of the dreams were more intimate encounters with three or four purposeful individuals who would rescue him from the bad guys and run him toward the river.

It was in these smaller groups he felt most comfortable, though his instincts told him there was safety in numbers. He began to think of Traveler and Gray John and Chief as his personal friends. He began to look forward to his dreams with what he thought might be unhealthy enthusiasm. They were his escape from reality. Just as the horses in his dreams helped him escape from the malicious Blue soldiers, the dreams themselves took him away from the daily tortures he was enduring as a "performance horse".

Junior won his classes easily at three small shows after placing second at Nolensville, but had yet to come up against Tim Sutton and his black again. They couldn't avoid each other forever, however, and the inevitable rematch took place east of Nashville not long before the Celebration. It was already August and it was hot and humid, typically uncomfortable for both horses and humans.

The horse show took place at night in front of the grandstand at a local county fair. Junior and his companions were hauled over in the afternoon and once again shown out of the trailer. One of the horses from Junior's barn was to be shown in the flat shod division. At first glance, these flat shod and "plantation" horses had it easy compared to Junior and the other performance horses. Their shoes were much lighter. They weren't standing on a stack of pads. They weren't allowed to show with chains. Junior just assumed they were in a lot less pain than he was. In some cases he might be right, especially at some of the newer "sound horse" organizations' shows where soundness is now the rule rather than the exception. In talking to this horse, whose name was Cisco, Junior realized he was in pure agony.

Junior remembered seeing Cisco being worked in the barn at home, but he thought he'd seen him wearing chains with stacks of pads on. Cisco told him he was right, he had had stacks and chains on at home. Sammy had changed his shoes just before the show.

"It's a weird feeling. I'm about five inches shorter, and when I move, my feet don't hit the ground when I expect them to," Cisco was saying. "When my front feet do hit the ground it hurts, it hurts a lot."

"Are they putting chemicals on you, under your leg wraps?" Junior asked.

"Oh yeah, they did that. They also did something to my hooves after they changed the shoes."

"What do you mean, Cisco?"

"Well, when the farrier trimmed my hooves he trimmed the outside supporting wall extra short so that the sole of my foot rests on the inside part of this wide ol' plantation shoe and takes the brunt of the pressure. There's even a little ridge along that inside part of the shoe that protrudes up into the tender part of my foot to add extra pressure. As if that wasn't enough, they put metal bands on these shoes that wrap around my hooves. These humans say the bands will help hold the shoes on. Well, hidden underneath each band is a row of metal screws that screw right into the sensitive insides of my hooves. They have loosened the screws for now until I go through inspection but I know they're gonna tighten them down real tight for the class, Junior. I just know it."

Cisco's class was just before Junior's, so they were in the inspection and warm-up area at the same time. He could see that his friend was not moving like a "pleasure" horse, but more like a performance horse. He was sore and he wasn't the only one. There was another horse in the flat-shod class that appeared very lame, almost as bad as Cisco. Junior found out later that this horse, trained by a man with the name of Ellis Walsh, had "spider line" wrapped and tightened around his coronet band to make him sore.

Junior wasn't able to watch the class, but as the horses exited the arena, he could see that Cisco won the class and the Ellis Walsh horse got second. The rest of the horses looked pretty sound to Junior, more like real pleasure or plantation horses, should look, natural. But the natural going horses didn't win these classes; the sorer the better, just like in his classes. No pain, no gain.

Sammy had Junior in top form for this show. He was reaching more now, flipping his front feet way out in front of him. Tim Sutton had his black colt ready too. Both trainers were looking forward to this meeting and neither one wanted to lose this close to the Celebration. The colts both passed inspection, and as the Hurricane Spray wore off, Junior and his counter-part began to show the effects of the intense training and soring they had endured. Even in the warm-up area it was shaping up to be a two-horse class again. Not that the other horses weren't as sore as these two, but Junior and the black colt had a beauty and a quality that shined through even the ugliness of the chemicals, big shoes, chains, and man-made gait.

Junior was the type of horse who could rise above his circumstances. That's what Chief had repeatedly told him in his dreams. He'd told him that he wasn't the kind of horse to be beaten, to be defeated by what these men were doing to him. He should be strong, be proud of his heritage. "Be bold and mighty forces will come to your aid," his friend had said. In the back of his mind, Junior wished he could fight back somehow, could turn things around. He wanted to; he just wasn't sure how to go about it. How could he change the world? Chief had said that if you try to change your own little part of the world, if you do your best, that's all you can do. But you have to try. If everyone did that, tried to make things right in their own little part of the world, eventually the world would change too, for the better.

"The thing is, Junior, if you do the best you can, even if you fail, you have actually succeeded. Just by trying you have made yourself and therefore the world better. So be strong, be bold, and don't ever give up."

Chief made a lot of sense for a horse that visited him in his dreams. Although Junior didn't always understand everything he was being told, Chief and the other spirit horses helped him get through this embattled life of his. When he was awake he had Old Timer to teach him. When he was sleeping, Chief, Traveler, Grey John, and the others were almost always there. Sometimes even after waking, Junior could still feel their presence.

He was in a lot of pain right now. Jeremy had just put the show chains on. Sammy was on his back. The warm-up was over. The Hurricane Spray evaporated. It was almost show time. As the chains rubbed on his sore legs and as Sammy dug his spurs into his side, Junior thought he saw Chief standing in the shadows, watching him. It comforted him to feel his spirit friend was there. He felt stronger already. He would get through this.

Earlier, he had watched Tim Sutton take his black colt through inspection, and thought he didn't look as sore as the last time they met. He didn't seem as sore as Junior himself felt. He had registered that observation in his mind and filed it away, not really knowing what to think of it. Sammy had noticed the same thing Junior had and was wondering what was going on. What did little Timmy have up his sleeve?

On the way up to the inspection, Sammy stopped Junior several times to push and probe, to make sure he would pass. There was always a lot of anxiety going through these inspections when you were constantly pushing the limit. Even though all the horses were sore, and almost all made it through inspection, Sammy did not want to be singled out again, to be made an example of. It was not a guilty conscience that sparked his anxiety; it was fear of getting caught.

Junior remembered how Old Timer had explained Sammy's nervousness before a class, leading up to the inspection.

"See, Junior, Sammy Lee and the other trainers, they break the law every day to do what they do. Sure, they get away with it most the time, but it's still against the law and there are penalties for breaking the law. Nowadays there are actually some fairly stiff penalties for soring horses, for abusing animals. They are rarely if ever applied, but they are there. Sammy and the other guys, they know that. It's kind of always hanging over their head that they might be busted, especially when the government men are around. Why do you think Sammy drinks so much?

"Of course, these people have built quite a protective little cocoon around what they are doing with all their lobbying, political contributions, and what not. Still, what they're doing is illegal and they're making a good living at it, which makes them criminals. Criminals have to learn to live with the possibility of getting caught, Junior, and paying a price. I also think that deep down some of these people actually may have a conscience and know what they're doing is wrong. They feel trapped by their circumstances. They can't get out. It's an, 'everybody does it, why should I be any different?' kind of thing. So, as one of them once said, they stick their heads in the sand and go on about their business."

Junior remembered how Chief had told him that one individual can make a difference. How you need to stand up for what is right. He wished that, if some of these people did have a conscience or maybe just a little horse sense, they could listen to Chief's advice.

Tim Sutton had been a little less anxious than Sammy Belford about going through this particular inspection. Sammy was right. He did have something up his sleeve. Actually, that something was a special pair of chains hanging on his equipment cart. After inspection and some preliminary warm-up, Tim's assistant put on a pair of gloves and removed the chains from the rack. These were what they called "hot chains" and the black colt soon found out why.

To lessen the risk of getting in trouble at the inspection station, Tim had figured out a way to put less soring chemicals on his horse before a show. He would put them on the chains, instead. Then, when the chemicals rubbed off the chains onto the animal's legs— instant results and ready to show. All of a sudden, the black colt was squatting and reaching, looking to beat Junior and Sammy once again. The hot chains, however, were not an exact science, and it was hard to judge just how much hot stuff to put on them. Soring was never an exact science, in fact, and Tim Sutton had always tended to err in the direction of too much rather than too little. Tonight was no exception.

Although the hot chains were not completely new to Junior's competitor, they did take him by surprise this evening. He had been feeling pretty good, not as sore as usual, until their class was about to begin. The chains changed all that in a big way. As Tim entered the ring to a roar from the crowd and yells of "Struttin' Sutton", it was all Tim could do to keep the big black colt from breaking out of the flat walk and double clutching with his front feet like he had before. He was beginning to realize he might have put too much juice on the chains. After a couple of rounds, the colt settled down into a pretty good groove. When the running walk was called Tim was able to send him on just enough to give the appearance of changing gaits. Maybe he was going to be all right after all.

One of the reasons Sammy and Tim had both entered their colts in this class was that it was a three-gait class. A canter would be required just as it would be in their class at the World Championship. They both needed a trial run, a good test for the colts before the big show, when so much was at stake. The canter, or slow gallop, is one gait natural to all breeds of horses and in most situations it is pretty much second nature. A natural, un-sored Walking Horse will most likely have a beautiful, easy going canter. In fact, before soring became so prevalent, the canter of the Tennessee Walking Horse was often touted as one of it's finest attributes, "like sitting in a rocking chair". As soring methods intensified and as the show walk of the horse became more man made, the canter became more difficult and less pleasing to perform for both horse and rider.

Junior hated to canter, which seemed strange to him. When he was younger he had loved to run. When playing with his friends he could take off at a nice little canter in a heartbeat. He could change leads, stop, and turn on a dime, then start right back into galloping across the field without even thinking about it. He thought about it now, though. Because to canter meant that he would be bringing one of his front feet down with a lot more force and weight behind it. Junior was sore. That meant that when his front feet met the ground it hurt. It hurt a lot, and that's what caused him to lift his legs higher and reach more. That was the whole theory behind the madness. His movements are pain-driven, unnatural. Well, putting extra weight on one of his sore feet was exactly what Junior did not want to do. Pain is to be avoided when at all possible.

What should be the most natural of all gaits to these horses has become very awkward, difficult, and painful for them to perform. Not only that, it can be very unpleasant to watch. As much as he hated to canter himself, Junior also hated to watch other show horses go through the ordeal. He could see the pain in their movements and in their eyes. Nevertheless, cantering was still a necessary evil to compete in certain classes. Although, the prevalence of two-gait classes at Walking Horse shows these days does indicate that it can be avoided more often than not. Junior was headed to a championship class at the Celebration, which still includes the canter as a required gait. For him, the dreaded canter could not be avoided.

When the announcer called for the third gait this first way of the ring, Junior felt his cue and acted accordingly. He hoped it wouldn't last long. They had practiced a lot at home and Junior actually had one of the more presentable canters in the class. You could see Sammy's arms pumping, though. His whole body language was concentrated toward keeping the colt in his gait. One of the more common reactions of a horse in too much pain to canter is to cross up with either his front or hind feet. Once one of these horses crosses up and his feet are landing out of sequence, it's almost impossible to get him back on track without coming completely out of the canter and basically starting over.

Struttin' Sutton was experiencing that now. He had gotten his colt to take the correct lead and fall into a canter, as unsightly as it was. But he had crossed up behind almost immediately. Tim had felt it when it happened, was hoping he was wrong but knew he was right. Besides, a buddy on the rail told him so. As he was approaching the turn he brought the colt back down to a flat walk, turned his head to the rail, and tried again. This time the same thing happened. After a few steps the colt crossed up behind. The trainer was getting angry now. He was running out of turn, where it was easiest to get the correct lead, and running out of time because the judge was bound to see him. He gave it one more try. The horse refused. He was getting mad, as well. Sutton tried to stay calm, one more try. This time the black colt took the lead just as they came out of the turn. The judge was now looking in their direction, and just as the colt started to cross up again, the judge turned his head. Tim knew he had dodged a bullet. He'd either been real lucky or the judge just didn't want to see his favorite horse mess up. He was hoping for the latter.

When the announcer called for the flat walk and reverse, both Sammy Lee Belford and Tim Sutton took the opportunity to rest their mounts. They reached over and adjusted their curb chains while hoping their horses would do as well the second way of the ring as they had the first. Tim was hoping the hot chains wouldn't get any hotter. He knew his black colt couldn't handle much more, especially in the canter. As he sent the colt back along the rail at a flat walk he thought he was moving a little easier. Was it just his imagination?

Junior and the black colt had similar ways of going. They were both big, strong, long legged colts. Junior was probably the prettier of the two, but the black was also a handsome colt. The edge on this night was Tim Sutton's use of the hot chains. His colt had a little more squat and a little more strut. What gave him the edge, however, could also be his downfall. And Tim knew it. In the running walk this second way of the ring both horses gave it all they had. Junior had a little more speed and overall a more fluid look. The black colt once again seemed to be doing more, but he could barely get out of a flat walk and was becoming rather jerky in his movements.

Just as it had been the last time they met, the crowd was evenly split. Sammy had seen his rival have trouble in the canter earlier and felt this could be the difference when the announcer asked the contestants to canter for the second time. Then, the unbelievable happened. Junior started out on the wrong lead. He was really hurting and when he took to cantering, he got confused and crossed up in front. He didn't want to come down on either front foot. Sammy was ready, though, and quickly stopped him, spurred him hard, and started him back up again. This time Junior took the correct lead and stayed in it.

Tim Sutton was not so lucky. His colt took a couple strange looking jumps, then took the bit in his mouth, set his jaw, set his mind, and refused to canter at all. All Tim could get him to do besides flat walk was hit a big trot for a couple steps. The big colt was mad and his mind was set. Tim tried all the way around the ring to get the colt to canter, then, realizing it would be the lesser of two evils, asked to be excused. At least this way he would remain undefeated. By "taking the gate" and leaving the competition, he could avoid being beaten by Sammy Lee and Junior. Sammy Lee Belford watched him leave and tried to keep from smiling.

NINE

Since it was technically still winter, weather at the Indio Date Festival was cold and sometimes foggy at night, though it warmed up quickly in the daytime. Socks got his first exposure to both camels and ostriches at Indio. He could not think of two more disagreeable members of the animal community. Camels would hiss and spit at you if you got too close. And, did they stink? Man! The big birds could also hiss and kick like a mule. Socks heard one of them stomping and kicking one day from three barns over. Both of these species were used at this particular horse show for racing around the arena to the delight of the crowd and the dubious entertainment of their appointed jockeys. The smell of rotting dates, the constant dust, the persistent flies, and those weird animals were to be some of Socks' fonder memories of Indio. Give him Santa Barbara anytime. Socks began to feel an unexplained uneasiness, similar to what Midnight must have felt at Del Mar that time. If there was anything to this sixth sense his mama had told him about, something bad was going to happen at this show.

Socks was no longer a junior horse this year. He had moved up into the tougher adult competition. And tougher it was. The West Coast trainers were getting away with more and more gimmicks and this was the year of the chain.

Royal Riggins was so adamantly against this new way of showing, he resisted to the last. He planned to show Socks with a pair of light leather "dog collars" that were actually just one-inch wide, half-inch thick leather straps. These were ultra light, lighter than any of the other horses could get away with. Socks could go light. That's probably one reason he had reacted so badly to his early soring days under Ellis Walsh. He was sensitive and natural going and Roy understood this.

Lacey and the others would be shown with heavier, weighted versions of the collar in order to stay competitive. The trainer would not show his horses with chains until absolutely forced to. To Roy this went against the very idea of "showing" a horse. Talk about a "bad image". He was at least fortunate at this show in that he had heard the esteemed lady who was this year's Date Festival judge voice similar opinions. She was a popular Saddlebred trainer and was noted for her work with young equitation riders. She was also on the board of editors of the prominent saddle horse magazine, Saddle and Bit. This magazine, although primarily a Saddlebred industry publication, had always given ample space to coverage of its sister Walking Horse industry. This was about to change, however. Chains, DQP's, obvious soring, and the rewarding of soring by more and more judges eventually forced Saddle and Bit to drop its Walking Horse coverage out of disgust and embarrassment.

Just as Saddle and Bit quit reporting on the Walking Horse industry, many of the major horse shows across the country eventually dropped their Tennessee Walking Horse performance classes. The Walking Horse classes had once been scheduled at the end of an evening's performance to help hold the crowd with their beauty and style. As the image and gait of the horse changed over the years, horse show managers realized the crowd favorite was becoming less and less so. At the multi-breed shows, many in the audience were repulsed by the increasing number of obviously sore and lame horses in these classes. They were doubly repulsed when the sorest horse in the ring was awarded the blue ribbon. Sore Walking Horse winners were roundly booed at the Los Angeles Forum, at the Cow Palace in San Francisco, and at other prominent horse shows across the country.

Royal Riggins felt good about his chances here at Indio, though. He had a good group of horses, an honest judge, and frankly, he had become quite accustomed to winning. He hoped that the changes affecting the industry could be held at bay for a little while longer. The bad guys were taking over, winning more battles, but they had yet to win the war. The arrests at Del Mar a few years earlier had been a stern warning to the infiltrators. Following the incident, the San Diego County chapter of the Humane Society did a three-page story on the Tennessee Walking Horse in their monthly newsletter, showing both the bad and the good. They showed close-ups of a horse's front feet ravaged by mustard oil, with hideous and permanent scars. They also displayed a picture of Roy riding Lacey as an example of the correct way of training and showing. The piece spoke at length on the expert and gentle approach of Royal Riggins and the beautiful and natural gait of this breed.

When Socks heard about the article, he was very proud of his friend Lacey and their trainer.

"That's really something, Miss Lacey, especially this day and age, for Walking Horses to be praised by the Humane Society. Of course, I don't know why I wasn't mentioned."

"I'm sure it was just a misprint, Socks. That you weren't mentioned, I mean."

"Must have been. Say, you remember how Midnight started having a bad feeling before those guys were arrested at Del Mar that time? Well, I think I'm feeling something like that now."

"Oh, really? Are you sure it's not just the camels and the ostriches getting to you?"

"I'm pretty sure. I feel like something bad is gonna happen to me this time, not just around me. What should I do about it?"

"I don't know that you can do anything about it. You just have to live your life, Socks. Take it as it comes. Be prepared. Keep an eye out. But in the end, you have to take what life brings you. You can't change your destiny. You can't change the world. You're just a horse, after all. Go with the flow, Socks, that's my philosophy. Don't take my word for it. Why don't you ask that old dog you're such good friends with? Maybe he can tell you what to do."

"Yeah, maybe ol' Midnight can help."

The next day Midnight responded to Socks' inquiries: "Lacey's right Snips. Some times these feelings are real vague, hard to pin down. Not always, mind you. I can tell a lot about a person in the first few minutes I meet them. I can tell if they're good to animals, if they like dogs, if they're a cat person. Premonitions now, they're more difficult. What's eating at you exactly?"

"I wish I knew. Something tells me it has to do with that night at Del Mar a few years back."

"You mean the night of the Fourth?" Midnight asked.

"Yep. I've got a strong feeling about that night and I haven't really thought about it in a while."

"You know that Sammy Belford is here in Indio, don't you? He's just one barn over."

"You're kidding. I didn't know that. Maybe that explains it. That's what I'm sensing, that he's here. That's why all the thoughts of Del Mar."

"Could be. He says he's cleaned up his act, not soring

anymore." Midnight said with a sneer.

"That'll be the day!"

"Hey, I agree. But at this show, and with this judge, he won't get away with much. My guess is he won't try."

"There's nothing he can do to me personally, is there?" Socks worried.

"Nah, you're just being paranoid. I think you're probably sensing the proximity of a dangerous man because of your experience with him, more than the sensing of any actual danger to you. Get my drift? Besides, what could he do to you?"

Yeah, I understand what you're saying. Go with the flow, like Lacey says, right?"

"Exactly, Snipper."

"You're not feeling anything negative like you did at Del Mar?"

"Well, nothing like at Del Mar, no. But I do get real negative whenever I spot that Sammy Belford or one of his ilk. I start right in to growling if I just get a whiff of that man. I'm not feeling any premonitions, if that's what you mean. Of course, that may not mean much because that premonition stuff can be real fickle sometimes, Socks. Sometimes it comes through loud and clear, and sometimes it doesn't come through at all."

"Great, you're a real comfort Midnight, my friend, a real comfort."

"That's why I'm here, mi amigo. Hey, you'll be all right. You're young and you like to talk. But deep down, I'll bet you're not as worried as you let on. You're an old soul, Socks, like me. I've heard you talk a lot about your heritage, about your ancestors. You've made a study of it. I can tell. You're one of the chosen ones. You're grounded. I predict a long and fruitful life for you. Not fruitful in the having lots of babies sense but in other ways. You'll be sowing seeds with your words, with your storytelling. You can help keep your heritage alive, Socks. That's important, especially with a breed like yours that's going through such drastic changes and facing an uncertain future."

"Wow, you trying to make me feel important, Midnight, so I won't worry about Sammy Belford? That's pretty heavy stuff you're laying on me there."

"I meant every word of it, Socks, and I think you know what I'm talking about. Like I said, you're young and you'll get smarter with age like me. Still, you have a gift for seeing the overall picture. I bet you sense that already. Someday you'll be comforting some young up-and-coming, just like I'm comforting you."

"Yeah, but you're a dog. I'm a horse. How can you know so much about me?"

"Well, you just answered part of that question yourself. I'm a dog, so I'm just naturally smart. Plus, I'm a dog named after a horse. Remember? Your grand-pappy, to be exact, and I was born in a stall. I've spent more time around horses in my long life than I have around other canines. So, I guess a little horse sense just comes natural to me by now."

Late that night, there was just a sliver of a moon, and the rows of tall date palms cast long and deep shadows over the barn area. Socks was awakened by two men slipping into his stall. One of the men talked to him reassuringly as he eased a leather halter over the horse's head. Socks was uneasy, but it all happened fast and he was still half-asleep, so he made little fuss. The man who had put the halter on him brought Socks to the middle of the stall and slipped the lead chain over his nose. This man held a flashlight aimed at his feet while the other man lifted the gelding's left front leg wrap and, with a well used eyedropper, started dropping oil of mustard on the front of Socks' pastern. With the first drop Socks knew what was going on and he started to squirm. He heard Midnight bark from the tack room two stalls down.

The flashlight left its target, and most of the caustic liquid fell harmlessly to the floor of the stall as Socks pulled back in fear.

He started kicking and pawing the air. The chain bit into the top of his nose and the men maneuvered reluctantly, but urgently, toward the stall door. As the first man exited, the second man quickly pulled the halter from Socks' head and slipped out the door, closing and latching it behind him. The burning sensation grew under his cotton leg wrap as the smell of oil of mustard filled his nostrils along with the smell of cheap whiskey and the unmistakable odor of Sammy Lee Belford.

Ricky Riggins wasn't exactly sure what it was when he first noticed the spot on Socks' leg. But his father knew and he had a strong suspicion of where it had come from, as well.

"Looks like they're trying to get a little revenge on us, Socks ol' boy. Sorry it had to be you. Ricky, go ahead and wash his legs real good. Put some salve on that blister and get him ready to ride. I'll work him without any action devices and see how he does. Did you see who did it, Midnight? Did you raise a ruckus and scare them off?" Royal asked the dog.

"Yeah, Mister Watchdog, my canine protector, what happened to you? I didn't hear you bark until the bad guys were practically out the door."

"I'm sorry Socks, I really am. I guess my hearing is just not what it used to be. I was off chasing rabbits somewhere across a beautiful green meadow, somewhere in dreamland, and didn't hear them coming. It's so peaceful in that dream place and my arthritis doesn't hurt me or slow me down. I'm younger, and faster, and so happy there. It's hard for me to come out of it sometimes. I hope you'll forgive me."

"Oh, I'll forgive you. I know you're not as young as you used to be. I just won't let you forget about it for a while."

Royal Riggins had started riding Socks recently with an old bit given him by S.W. Beech years before. It was a basically standard Saddlebred type of curb bit with a straight shank and a low port. S.W. had used the bit on Black Angel, the great show mare of the 1940's. Black Angel had won the Walking Horse Grand Championship in 1943 wearing this bit.

When Socks learned the history of the bit, it filled him with pride. Black Angel was eventually retired to breeding, and S.W. made a present of the bit to his young friend and protégé, Royal Riggins. Roy tried the bit out on the young stud colt his father-in-law bought from Beech. As a result, they won the Pacific Coast Championship in 1950. Roy later used the bit on several of his favorite West Coast winners, including a full brother to Hill's Perfection, a mare named April Love, Special Sonata, and eventually Socks. The trainer even kept this special bit of history until long after his retirement, periodically cleaning and polishing the stainless steel apparatus that was the link between man and horse, between hands and mouth, and holding it in high esteem. The bit became a symbol to him of the history of the Tennessee Walking Horse as he had known it from the 1940's to the present.

But, this special bit was not working with Socks today. The mustard blister on his left front was causing Socks to go unevenly and to pull a little on one side of the bit. His left front was reaching slightly higher and farther than his right. They had put plenty of salve on the injury, but Roy was afraid to use even the lightest pair of dog collars on the horse. The leather straps were normally harmless, but with all of the sand and grit present in the footing even they might aggravate the blister, which somehow needed to heal by tonight when Socks had his first class. Roy decided to try a trick his friend and mentor, Winston Wiser, had shown him. He thought if it would help at all, it would work better with a more flexible bit, so he changed Socks' bridle.

The bit he put in the horse's mouth was the short-shank, broken mouth-piece bit Roy had worked him with for years, before switching to the Black Angel bit. Socks was more than familiar with the new bit. Roy undid the reins, crossed them underneath the horse's neck, and brought them back on top. He didn't re-buckle them, just in case he had to switch them back real quick.

As Royal first stepped him out, Socks was confused. He wasn't sure which way he was supposed to go. Roy took him slowly, gave him direction. Socks thought he understood, though he was still hesitant. He moved forward with increasing speed up to a fast flat walk. He continued to lean on one side of the bit to correspond with his uneven stride, but Roy had tricked him by crossing the reins. Left was right and right was left and, without actually being aware of it, Socks slowly began to ease off the left side of the bit and even out his stride. Turning was tricky and was accomplished with a little neck reining, a little leg pressure, and a lot of will power. He used the rail to help give the colt guidance and security.

Royal Riggins was the kind of natural horseman who, as a man of few words, would have a hard time articulating every move he made in the saddle. Yet he instinctively knew exactly where each one of a horse's legs was at any point in time and exactly what his appropriate response should be. His hand and body language was dictated by his subconscious and by instinct, rather than by any over-evaluative thought process. This little trick of the crossed reins was something he used from time to time, and he hoped it would help in this instance, but it was by no means a cure-all. He would never suggest to anyone else that they ride with the reins crossed like this. It was too dangerous, especially for amateurs, and it didn't always help.

Luckily, it did seem to help Socks some, and he worked the gelding with the reins crossed until he became more level in front and lost the little hitch in his hind end. Hopefully, by this evening's class the blister would have healed enough to be less of a problem and he could go back to riding with uncrossed reins. That would be much safer in a ring full of horses, in case Socks got his signals crossed. Meanwhile, he needed to find Dr. Will and apprise him of the situation.

TEN

"**L**ooks like a mustard drop, all right," said the good doctor. "You say he's going unevenly? That's not surprising. Guess you're lucky there wasn't more damage."

"They had to get in, do the deed, and get out, Will. Slither in under the door, bite him on the leg, and slither back out into the night. Just like a snake." Roy said.

"Yeah, Sammy the Snake." Ricky chimed in.

"Now, Son, we don't know for sure who did this. We can't prove anything."

"Is there any doubt in your mind, Dad?"

"Well no, but that's just between us, between you and me and Dr. Will here. We can't go accusing anybody unless we have proof. Unless ol' Socks himself can tell us who it was or unless somebody besides he and Midnight saw them, we've got to watch what we say. Understood?"

"Yes, sir."

"The best way for us to react to this is to act like nothing happened. That will get their goat more than anything. Can we pass inspection tonight, Doc?"

"I think so. Since it's just on one side like this and since I, too, have a pretty good idea what happened here, I think you'll get in. Are you sure you want to try to show this horse tonight? Down here with this sandy soil, unless that blister heals up super fast, you'll have a hard time putting any kind of action device on him without causing irritation and possible bleeding. Then, besides causing him to go unevenly, either I, or the judge, would have to excuse you. Those guys, Sammy the Snake and his cronies, would love that, Roy. They'd say, 'look at that Royal Riggins. He's just like the rest of us. Now he's in trouble, too.' This spot might even break out without a chain or dog collar in this sand. Why not just wait a few days to show the horse? It would be a lot safer. Scratch him from tonight's class and show him later in the week."

"I know what you're saying, Will. But you know how bull headed I am. Whoever did this probably knew Socks was supposed to show tonight and figured I would either not show him, or I'd try to and it would lead to trouble. Well, they're not going to get what they want, not from me."

"You are bull headed. But it's your call. Like I said, the way it looks now, you'll make it past inspection. After that, no guarantees."

"All right, Will. Thanks for stopping by. We'll see you later tonight." Roy turned to his son.

"Ricky, where's the black shoe polish?"

"It's in the middle trunk. Top right, I think."

"Good boy. Now let's get to work."

"I still think we ought to march right over there and confront him to his face. 'Sammy the Snake,' the name fits."

"I know what you're feeling, Son, believe me. Part of me wants to go over there and tear his head off. But that wouldn't get us anywhere. We're gonna take the high road on this one. Be patient. Now get me that can of green salve, the one that's almost empty."

Ricky brought the can of salve his dad requested, then Roy proceeded to add a little of the black shoe polish to the ointment, mixing it with a screwdriver. He stirred it up well, and then added a little more polish until the color was where he wanted it. The two compounds were of similar texture and mixed well together. When it looked good to him he went to Socks' stall and put some of the mixture on the horse's blister. It was a perfect match. He rubbed it in gently, careful not to aggravate the sore, and left a liberal amount to soak in.

"Go ahead and put his leg wraps on now, Rick. The cotton will absorb the extra goop. As long as it keeps healing we should be all right tonight, especially with the extra camouflage. It's a good thing they weren't able to get anymore mustard on there than they did."

After his afternoon nap, Midnight relieved himself on a date palm and went sniffing around Socks' stall door.

"Go away, you mangy mutt."

"Aw, come on. Is that anyway to talk to your canine protector, your guardian angel dog? I was just checking up on you, making sure you're all right."

"Yeah, I'm all right, no thanks to you."

"Hey, I barked at the bad guys."

"Uh huh, just as they were leaving, to say goodbye. After I'd already been held captive and tortured."

"'Held captive and tortured,'" Midnight laughed. "Horse, you do have a way with words."

"I thought you'd like that. So what's the verdict? Think I'll show tonight? I feel pretty good, actually. That green salve works great. I can almost feel the blister going away. Actually, I think those men meant to do me more harm than they did. Maybe something did scare 'em off."

"Well, if you'll let me answer your question. Yes, I think

you'll probably show tonight the way they've been talking. Now, I've got to finish my rounds. See ya later."

Socks was given a smaller portion of hay for his afternoon feeding than usual, part of the routine when he had a class that night. So, he was just a little hungry and somewhat apprehensive about the upcoming event when Royal and Ricky arrived from the hotel that evening.

"You going to show him with the little leather straps, Dad, or go with the medium dog collars?"

"Neither one."

"Neither one? What will you use, then?"

"Nothing, Ricky, nothing at all. I don't want to take the chance of irritating that blister."

"Yeah, but nothing? Will he be able to do enough to compete? All the other horses will be wearing chains."

"He may lose something on the front end, might not have quite as much action. But I think he'll do enough, especially if I ride him on a little. Socks is real natural. If any horse can do this, he can. I really think we can pull it off, Rick. Especially with Miss Helen as the judge. She's been real vocal against what's been happening to the Walking Horse industry, showing with chains in particular. Showing Socks bare legged may actually be to our advantage. I haven't shown a horse this way in over twenty years, so it will be fun. Where'd you put the...oh, here they are."

The inspection that night went on almost without a hitch. Socks made it through just fine. You couldn't see the blister at all from a distance and it was even hard to make out up close. The shoe polish and salve mixture had soaked in enough, and been dabbed enough times by Ricky and Roy, that none of it came off on Dr. Will's hands. Socks could see Sammy and his buddies staring at his legs wondering where they'd gone wrong, why there wasn't more visible damage. Socks did have a very slight hitch in his git-a-long when Roy first got on him. The trainer quickly rode him down an aisle between the barns to try and work him out of it. Sammy was too busy getting his own mount through inspection, concentrating on Dr. Will, to notice Socks' apparent unevenness. But one of his cronies had never taken his eyes off Socks, and later reported to Sammy what he had seen.

Belford's horse was a big-boned sorrel that moved stiff-legged and slow, and who Dr. Will was sure had been sored quite often in the past but was fairly presentable at the moment. Sammy Lee was apparently showing a little respect for the good doctor and a little street smarts, too, by laying off of the chemicals some. He had assured his customers that he would stay out of trouble, that their horses would pass inspection here at Indio. If they didn't, he would blame it on the veterinarian, of course.

This time at least, his horse got the okay from Dr. Will. Socks wasn't the only horse with a hitch this night. Sammy's sorrel was at times going noticeably higher with his right front and hitching behind to catch up. He was showing him with eight-ounce chains, the maximum weight allowed. When the Belford entry entered the ring he had evened out, but Sammy was jerking his hands every which way, making it obvious to everyone he was really in the horse's mouth. Miss Helen, the Kentucky Saddlebred judge and equitation instructor, did not like the way he was riding, or the way the sorrel's back end was so creepy-crawly, his hocks so low to the ground. But he was walking and doing a lot, and she knew she'd have to do something with him. There were only three other horses in the class so far and they were kind of mediocre horses, she thought, though they were sound.

In came Royal Riggins on pretty boy Socks with no chains, no dog collars or bell boots, no action devices at all. The last ones to enter the ring, they came in at what was really a running walk, letting it all hang out. Roy slowed Socks to a fast flat walk – the required gait of entry – by the time they reached the turn, but not after making quite an impression on everyone, including the judge. No one could ever say Royal Riggins was not a showman.

Judge Helen liked Socks. He wasn't doing quite as much – action wise – as the big sorrel of Sammy Belford's, but he presented a better overall picture, much more natural. He was nodding his head and walking, and he was bare legged. Although this was not an equitation class, she couldn't help but notice the huge difference in riding styles of the two trainers. Royal Riggins sat tall in the saddle, straight backed, hands held low and together, his upper body just floating along on the back of his horse. Sammy Lee Belford, on the other hand, was hunched over, head bobbing with that of his horse. His feet were through the stirrups with toes pointed down, heels in his horse's flanks. His hands were too high and wide apart, never still, always jerking. She had to remind herself this was not an equitation class, back to business.

Socks' blister had healed quickly and in another day or so probably wouldn't be a factor at all. Since the sore was on his left front if he were going to have any trouble, it would be this first way of the ring, going counter-clock wise. He had handled the cross-reined business with maturity, but was glad to have things back to normal and he liked showing barelegged. Roy was helping Socks stay even with his hands, picking him slightly with his fingers, but nothing so obvious that anyone noticed. Communication between horse and rider was so good that he never missed a step. When the announcer asked for the horses to canter, Socks displayed a beautiful, natural canter, a real rocking chair. Sammy's poor sorrel's canter was painful to watch. He was all strung out and jerky compared to Socks. When the class was called to reverse, and the rest of the riders took a moment to let their mounts catch their breath, Roy patted Socks on the neck and told him he'd done a good job. The hard part was over.

Roy and Socks were the second ones back on the rail. They started out a few lengths behind Bob Fields and his gray, but quickly passed them. Socks felt great, and Roy was riding him on just a bit more than usual to make up for the lack of action devices. This extra urging really perked the horse up, and he began showing better the second way of the ring. Sammy Lee's horse, on the other hand, was having trouble this way. His hitch was back and getting worse. On their first pass in front of the judge in this direction, Sammy was able to jerk and spur and somehow cajole the big sorrel into staying fairly even. It was all down hill from there. Judge Helen was not just watching one spot on the rail, either. It was a small class and she would turn around and watch different horses at different locations. This was not her first horse show, after all. The woman knew what she was doing. On the backside, she saw the sorrel noticeably hitching – limping, really. The longer the class went, the worse the horse got.

During the first way of the ring, the judge had been wondering if she might have to tie this big sorrel with the sore way of going. She'd seen this kind of Walking Horse before. Whether or not he had actually had chemicals applied immediately before the class, he moved like it because he'd been sored so much in his life that he didn't know any other way to move. He couldn't look natural, not like Socks and the other horses in the class.

And what about that Roy Riggins showing his horse barelegged just like it was twenty years ago? She loved it. That's the way these horses should be shown. Miss Helen signaled the announcer to ask the riders to bring their mounts to the center of the ring and line up. As she walked around Socks, judging his confirmation, she told Roy she wished they would all go back to showing that way. Roy tipped his hat, and with a big grin said: "Me, too." He wanted to say more, but kept it to himself.

Roy and Socks won the class to huge applause and, once again, Socks was the talk of the show. Bob Fields was second on his little gray. Alec Perez tied third, Jan Mussleman fourth, and a steaming Sammy Lee Belford got the fifth place ribbon. His horse's unevenness had gotten so bad, last place was the only place judge Helen could put him. Back at their barn, Sammy and the sorrel's owners put their own spin on things.

"Can you believe that? I swear! Ol' Riggins has all these Saddlebred judges in his pocket! Another class rigged by Riggins. 'Riggin' Riggins' that's what his name oughta be. That gelding of his wasn't doing nothin' but just a-pacing around the ring, barely coming off the ground in front. What a joke! We need to get some real Walking Horse judges out here and some real inspectors, somebody that understands these horses, not some ol' pet vet. The time will come, I swear it will."

That night after the show Sammy's clients, the people who owned the big sorrel, accosted Miss Helen. They didn't physically attack her. But for a moment, she wasn't so sure they weren't intending to.

"Well, you did what you came here to do, didn't you?" One of them asked rather loudly.

She tried to ignore them, pretended she didn't hear what the woman said. But they persisted: "I said you did what you came here to do, didn't you!"

She kept walking toward the parking lot, but without stopping, said: "I have no idea what you're talking about. Now I must go. Goodnight."

ELEVEN

Rain was coming down so hard that Junior could barely see the horse tethered next to him. He knew it was Traveler, though. Beyond him was Chief. Gray John was there, and so was Black Angel. Sammy, Jeremy, and some other men were huddled around what used to be the campfire. As in most of these dreams, the men got up from around the fire and approached the captive horses. While the other men restrained and positioned them, Jeremy produced his dreaded paintbrush and can, and began slopping the scootin' juice on the horses' front legs. Then came the plastic wrap and outer leg wraps to hold the chemicals in. Junior was hoping that the pouring rain would wash some of the stuff away, but no such luck. The pain was familiar and expected, but never welcome. He just wanted to jump out of his skin.

The men went back to the washed-out fire. Jeremy threw the remainder of the nasty, blue – now turned to red – liquid on the rain-soaked coals and they burst into flames. The men erupted in laughter – that evil, frightening laughter that haunted Junior even in his waking hours at times. While Junior shuddered at the sound, Chief was busy untying the horses' ropes. He quickly went down the line, and in short order they were all free and running down that familiar road toward the river. The war horses, Traveler and Gray John, led the way, followed closely by Chief and Black Angel. Junior was bringing up the rear, trying to catch up. His legs were killing him. The pain was slowing him considerably and he was bogging down in the mud when he heard the riders behind them. The bad guys were gaining ground and there were more of them now. Chief and Black Angel slowed their pace and came along side him, one on either side.

"You have to keep going, Junior. Don't give up. That's what they want you to do," Chief told him over the sound of the rain and thunder.

"They want you to accept the pain, let it change you, make you something you're not," he heard Black Angel say. "Don't let it. You have to fight. Fight it with all your heart and keep running to the river."

Junior could hear Sammy Lee and the other riders gaining on them. Traveler and Gray John slowed and turned toward the approaching riders.

"You all keep going. We'll stay here and see if we can't slow them down some," Traveler said in that commanding voice of his.

"But you're out numbered! I won't leave you." Junior cried.

"You must go on, Junior! We're doing this for you. Don't you understand? You must make it to the river. Chief and Black Angel will go with you. John and I will stay here and make a stand. Don't worry. We won't be alone."

No sooner were the words out of his mouth than Junior noticed other horses coming out of the woods, riderless horses, many of whom he recognized. He saw Roan Allen, Merry Legs, Midnight Sun, and even Allan. Junior wasn't sure how he knew all these horses, but he did. They were all there for him. They were there to fight off the bad guys so that he could escape. He couldn't believe it; Bald Stockings, Brooks, Tom Hal, King Phillip, General Lee's Traveller, all these famous horses, coming together for him. What was going on? He wanted to stay and fight if there was to be a battle. He felt inspired by the presence of these great spirit horses. But his battle was to reach the river and swim to the other side. They all made that very clear. Somehow, that was what was important above anything else. So he continued onward, down the road and across the field, toward the river with Chief and Black Angel leading the way.

That's when he was rudely awakened. Jeremy led Junior to the wash rack where his bandages were removed and his legs were washed and dried. He wasn't going to be ridden today but Sammy wanted to try out a new chemical on his young prospect.

For years now, the presence of plastic food wrap has become increasingly obvious at Walking Horse barns and shows across the country. It is vital to the soring methods used to train these show horses, or as they are often called, "performance horses". The plastic wrap helps "sweat" the chemical irritants into the animal's body, intensifying their effect and lessening the visible damage to the surface hair and skin. It is also a dead give away that the user is soring his or her horse, since that is it's main function and purpose. Tack and supply stores that cater to Tennessee Walking Horse customers sell plastic wrap in high volume, even at horse shows, under the noses of federal inspectors. No group of exhibitors of any other breed of horse has need of this product at all, much less in so much volume. No other group keeps large supplies of plastic wrap on hand in their barns and at shows. Plastic wrap can be seen sticking out underneath the leg wraps of horses at the shows from weanlings on up. As has happened in the past, the fear of getting caught is the mother of invention, and Walking Horse trainers are nothing if not inventive.

A friend of Sammy Lee's, an older man named Ellis Walsh, told him how to avoid using plastic wrap.

"It's called collodion, Sammy. It does the same thing as the plastic, works just as good, but it's invisible. It's a liquid, a chemical sealant. You just paint it on over your other stuff and that's that. But be careful, it can be dangerous. They make the stuff from guncotton and ether, so it can be explosive. You don't want to breath the fumes, or get too much of it on you. It dries real quick, so you can put your regular leg wraps over it. The main thing is you don't have to mess with all that darn plastic wrap and these nosey do-gooders can't say, 'Look at all that plastic. They use it to sore their horses.'"

So, Junior had yet another chemical applied to his body. He was having more and more stomachaches and headaches. It was Old Timer's theory that all of these chemicals were at the bottom of such ailments.

"As old as I am, I don't have half the problems you do, Junior."

"I have had my share of aches and pains lately. You know, I hate to be a complainer, Old Timer, but I feel like I'm getting old before my time. I don't know if I'll ever make it to that ripe ol' age you have. Whatever it is."

"Don't be so sure Junior. It's hard to tell about such things. Why, when I was your age, I never dreamed of living to be this old."

Junior tried to picture Old Timer as a young horse, strong and full of energy, like he'd seen him in his dream. He wished he knew more about the old horse's past, what his life had been like. Had he faced some of the same trials Junior was facing? He had learned a lot about the history, and lineage, and some of the problems of their breed from his old friend. But as much as he liked to talk, the old one hadn't shared much of his own personal history. The next day, Junior was about to ask Old Timer to tell him his story when the stall door slid open.

"Let's go, Junior. You've got a big day ahead of you. The

horseshoer's here and I think they're gonna make some changes, fix you up right," said William.

"That's all I need!" Junior thought. He had come to dread changes and fear surprises. They almost always meant more agony for him. It seemed that new and different forms of torture were constantly being dreamed up by these cruel men who had control over his life. They must spend a lot of time thinking these things up. Why couldn't they just leave him alone for once?

Junior was led to the breezeway where the farrier had just finished working on one of his stablemates. The pungent odor of clipped and burning hoof hung in the air as a reminder of atrocities just rendered, and as a harbinger of those to come. Junior's eyes were as wide as saucers when he stepped onto the ribbed concrete between the crossties with the trepidation of a seasoned – if not voluntary – soldier.

The farrier's assistant began removing the oversized shoes and pads from Junior's hooves as his employer and Sammy Lee Belford discussed what was to be done. Sammy Lee felt pressured by the competition, especially Tim Sutton, to try to take Junior's performance up a notch. He also needed to avoid anymore scarring of the colt's legs, if possible. He decided to try something that was risky but had worked for him in the past.

"What I'd like to do, Carter, is something like we did to Accelerator a while back. I know it's risky, but we got a World Championship out of it. I think it might work on this colt."

"You mean you want to put a spring and ball bearing in there between the pads and his frog area? Come on, Sammy, you know that stuff shows up on the floroscope that the government men use now. You can't do that anymore, at least not at any shows with USDA inspectors like The Celebration."

"Yeah, I know. But they won't be at this next little show we're going to and I need to get this colt to do more. I like what those springs and ball bearings do. Let's go ahead and put them in there for now. We'll try to figure something else out for the Celebration. Besides, having that stuff in there for a while aught to have some sort of lingering effect after we take it out, don't you think?"

"Oh yeah, it will Sammy. He'll be real tender. And, I tell ya, I've been wondering about this product us horseshoers use a lot now. This company makes a flexible sole pack, a hoof builder, and a super fast adhesive. But it's the adhesive I've been meanin' to tell you about. It gets hard as a rock in about two minutes and it stays that way. It comes in this little tube here and I could shoot it right up in his sole. Got this little gun that goes with it. Works like a caulking gun."

"Is that right?"

"Yeah, and it would never show up on no damn inspection machine, either. You could put it right in there where you put your spring and ball bearing. Take them out and put this stuff in right before the big show. It'd be like having a big ol' jagged rock in his foot."

"And it won't show up, you're sure?"

"Yes Sir. Sure as I'm standin' here."

"Carter, I think you might be on to something there. Yes sir, you just might be on to something." The assistant finished removing Junior's shoes and pads. The horse felt odd standing there without the artificial height of his show horse "build-ups". He hated to admit it, but he almost missed them. He was so used to walking around with all that stuff on his feet that he felt strangely uncomfortable without it. Maybe it was like Traveler said. If you let them do these things to you long enough, eventually, gradually, you learn to accept it.

What was done to him next would have been hard for any horse to accept and Junior's desire to fight back was strong, but so were the restraints. William had run the chain of the lead shank under his chin and, with Jeremy's help, had twitched the tip of

Junior's nose to take his attention away from the farrier and his drill.

After trimming the colt's hoof short, but in a fairly normal manner, Carter attached a one and a half inch wood bit to his electric drill while Jeremy gave Junior an injection of ace promizine. The farrier picked up Junior's left front foot and placed it between his knees. He then asked his assistant to hand him the drill. The sound penetrated Junior to the bone. He jumped and, despite his handlers' efforts, broke free momentarily from the farrier's grasp. Carter gave the colt a brutal kick to the gut accompanied by a barrage of profanity; then, after stretching his back, bent down and picked up the hoof for another attempt. This time Junior was held in place as the drugs kicked in.

Holes were drilled in the frog area of Junior's hooves, making room for the ball bearing and the high-tension spring, which were then cemented into place. While one man drilled the hole in Junior's hoof, another kept spraying the area with a cauterizing spray to keep it from bleeding. Carter's assistant mixed a small amount of cement to fill in the hole and hold the spring and bearing in place. Then, more plastic pads were nailed to those already in place to seal the contraption. The large shoe was tacked on and a metal band was strapped around Junior's hoof to help hold everything together. He was ready to go. After his legs were medicated and wrapped, the dazed colt was returned to his stall.

Once again, Old Timer watched what was going on with sadness and with anger. He really had an affinity for the young bay stallion. Junior reminded him of another young bay he had known years before, a stallion who had become kind of a hero figure to the old horse and to many others, as well.

"You know, Junior, I've told you a lot of stories about the horses responsible for this breed of ours and some of the events of the past, but..."

"Oh, gee, Old Timer I don't know if I'm in the mood to listen to any stories right now. I'm still kind of groggy and I hurt so much, my ears are ringing."

"I know you're hurting, Son, but that's why I'm talkin' at you, to take your mind off. Well, what I was about to say was that I know I've talked a lot about our breed's history but I haven't told you much about my own past. I guess I figure in the over all scheme of things, my life ain't as important as the ones I've been telling you about."

"Oh, all right. I would like to hear you talk about yourself some. In fact, I've been looking forward to hearing more about your life, Old Timer. You could start by telling me just how old you are. That is, if you know."

"Well now, Junior, I'm not sure that is the most polite question you could have asked me. I could lie and say I really don't know. But the truth is, I do have a pretty good idea how old I am. Let's just say I'm thirty-something and leave it at that."

"Thirty-something? Can't you be more specific?"

"How specific do you want? Old is old, and thirty-something is old."

"Yeah, you're right. Wow, you are old!"

"Well now, we both already knew that, didn't we? Before I start talking too much about myself, seems I remember telling you about some of the early show horses like Roan Allen, and Merry Legs, and Merry Boy, Midnight Sun, Black Angel. I tell you about them, Junior?"

"Yes, you did. And, I love those stories, but..."

"One of my favorite horses from that time was a gelding named Talk Of The Town. He was by Midnight Sun and out of Merry Rose. So he and my daddy were half-brothers, Junior. Well, Talk was a gelding, like me, and he won the World Grand Championship three times, three years in a row in the early 1950's. No horse before or since has accomplished that feat. And I believe he was the last gelding to win the championship.

"Talk's road to fame was not an easy one, Junior. He changed hands a half dozen times and was sold once for two hundred dollars. But, eventually, he fell into the capable hands of Mr. Steve Hill who rode him to all three of his big wins in Shelbyville. Steve Hill was one of the last of the old breed of trainers, training Walking Horses before chemicals came into the picture. He was the good friend of a man who was lucky enough to get to train yours truly for a while. He was also the friend and contemporary of a man who was one of the greatest trainers of all time, Winston Wiser.

"Winston Wiser won the World's Grand Championship two years in a row in the fifties, just one year after Talk Of The Town won it three times with Steve Hill up. His mount was the beautiful and famous Go Boy's Shadow. Shadow looked a lot like his sire, Merry Go Boy, who was by ol' Merry Boy and who also won the big stake twice with Winston Wiser in the saddle. You still with me, Junior?"

"Still here, Old Timer. Keep talking."

"Well, Merry Go Boy was foaled in 1943 and under Mr. Wiser's fine tutelage, he won the weanling championship that very year. The next year, he won the yearling championship. The next year – under saddle of course – he won the two-year old championship. And as a three year old, he was the junior champion. When he was four, he won the Grand Championship of the World, and again the next year."

"Did the horse ever lose?"

"Not hardly, my young friend. Not only did he never lose when he was shown, but he went on to be one of the greatest sires of show horses there ever was. Evidence of that was his son, Go Boy's Shadow, who in turn became a great sire of champions. As far as I can tell Junior, from what I've picked up around here, you have a good amount of Go Boy's and Shadow's blood running through your veins."

"Are you sure, Old Timer? How do you know?"

"Yeah, I'm pretty sure you could trace yourself back to ol' Shadow and his daddy, from what I've heard. You've got the look. You're bigger, of course, than they were, but you've still got that short-backed, strong-shouldered, Morgan-look, just a larger version of it."

"You mean you think I look like Justin Morgan?"

"Well, not exactly. But you most likely do have a trace of his blood running through your veins, and so do I. Now, those two ancestors of yours I was talking about, Go Boy and Shadow, they showed more of the Morgan characteristics than you 'cause they were closer to the source. You know what I'm sayin'? Even I am related to some fine Morgan horses, just a few generations back.

"I guess I'm just kind of ramblin' again, Junior, and I do apologize. But since we're talking about the way you look, you remind me an awful lot of a horse I knew a long time ago in another place, seems like another world. He was a big, strong bay stallion like you with a thick neck and a Morgan head on him. He was the kind of horse you run into once in awhile that is real good at getting in trouble. He was restless. He was always playing with things with his mouth, with his feet. When we'd go to horse shows the humans would always put some sort of extra snap or chain on his stall door because he could open just about anything. He could untie any knot a man could make, Junior. His name was Chief."

Chief? Could it be that the horse Old Timer was talking about was the same Chief Junior knew in his dreams, the horse that was always helping him and giving him guidance and advice? The description fit, "big, strong bay stallion with a thick neck and a Morgan head on him." It didn't seem possible. But there it was. Old Timer was describing perfectly his friend Chief. The horse who, along with Traveler, was his spiritual advisor of sorts. It was Chief, after all, who was always untying the knots and freeing him from the tethers of the devil soldiers. It made perfect sense and yet was perfectly insensible.

Junior had been about to doze off when Old Timer began talking about Chief. The old horse's ramblings, as interesting as they were, often had this effect on him. Part of him wanted desperately to hear more about this horse named Chief that Old Timer said he had known. The other part couldn't wait to fall asleep and cross over into that other world, the dream world, the spirit world, that he was more and more dependant on to take him away from this world of constant sorrow in which he lived. The call was irresistible. He knew his friends were waiting for him. He would probably have to face the awful soldiers who so closely resembled the men he knew here in this life. But he knew he could count on Traveler and Chief and the others to rescue him. They always did. Junior felt somehow, in the back of his brain, that these mystic friends of his were teaching him something, something valuable, something he needed to know to survive.

TWELVE

"**I** don't see how they're gonna beat him now, Sammy."

"Yeah, he's strokin' Sammy Lee."

"Yeah, but he don't wanna canter much after that last shoeing job. Let's make him do it one more time each way. You come behind me with the bullwhip, and crack him good. Keep after him. Don't let him fall out."

Junior was trying to catch his breath and trying not to think of the pain. He felt the presence of Chief and Traveler. They were standing in the shadows at the end of the barn. He knew they were there to give him encouragement, to help him hold on to some thread of hope, some possible chance of deliverance. But his hopeful, helpful friends, as real as they seemed, were just figments of his imagination, weren't they? What was real was Sammy Belford on his back and Jeremy and William and the other men on the ground who were relentlessly determined to torture him on a daily basis.

Spurs in his side, Junior stepped out away from the huddle of men in the middle of the barn as his trainer headed him towards the end where he thought he had seen his spirit friends standing a short time ago. As Sammy turned the colt at the end of the barn, he cued him to canter. If Junior even thought about balking he didn't think long because Jeremy was lashing his legs with the long cracking whip he knew all too well. He did what the men wanted him to do in both directions and on the correct leads, without crossing up. Despite the pain in his feet and lower legs, the spurs and the whip made cantering correctly the lesser of evils to the young stallion.

It seemed like he was almost always making the choice, whether consciously or subconsciously, to do something because it was the lesser of evils. Junior's training, the whole theory behind it, the primary motivation for his movements, was pain – all stick and no carrot. The gaits that Junior and others like him were being taught to perform were totally driven by this.

One of the men in the barn today was Ellis Walsh. This man had been training for a long time from what Junior could gather. The other men seemed to show him respect, listen to his opinions. Even Sammy treated the older man with deference. Though they were technically competitors, these two were rarely in direct competition anymore. In the last few years, Ellis had slimmed down his training operation considerably. He was now specializing in plantation and "pleasure" horses. Ellis Walsh was passing himself off to the uninformed as the gentle old trainer of the past who wouldn't sore his horses, who believed in training the old-fashioned way.

"Don't let him fool you, Junior," Old Timer told his friend when the men put the colt back in his stall. "He is one of the worst. Old Ellis seems real friendly and likable, even jovial. He acts like he loves his horses, but it's just that, Junior, an act. Why, he's the one who showed Sammy Lee that awful trick with the ball bearing and spring they have pulled on you. Now that he's specializin' in these so-called pleasure horse classes, it's made him even more inventive. Since they can't show those horses with pads or chains, he has come up with some very painful, hidden ways of sorin' 'em. Guys like Ellis Walsh, believe me, Junior, the horse world is not a better place with them in it."

"You sound like you know him pretty well, Old Timer."

"That I do, Junior, that I do. Old Ellis and I go way back. 'Course, like I said, he has gotten more inventive over the years, like most of these trainers. Why, he's been caught counter-sinkin' nails and screws in horses' hooves, into the quick, and coverin' them up with cement and wood putty. Most all his horses have been road foundered at some time or other and he does his best to contract their heels to where its real painful. He's real good at usin' Spider Line, wrappin' it around the coronet band so tight it sinks in to where it's hard to detect, and it hurts like hell."

"What's Spider Line, Old Timer?"

"Spider Line is a very thin fishin' line that is also very, very strong. It's so thin that it's hard to see, yet you could reel in a Marlin with it. I've heard magicians use it to levitate people. Well, Walking Horse trainers use it too. I knew a horse not too long ago that almost lost her hooves due to that stuff. A trainer named Thompson, or Johnson, or somethin' like that, sold this mare to the people that owned me for a while. Well, anyway, this trainer had been usin' Spider Line on the mare as one of his "trainin'" methods, and when he sold her he forgot to take it off. Maybe he left it there on purpose, I don't know. I hope not 'cause she was the sweetest old mare you could ever know and what happened to her no one deserves. See, the people that bought her, Junior, they didn't know that wire was down there cuttin' off the circulation and diggin' into her flesh. By the time they figured out what was happenin', it was almost too late. The vet had a heck of a time diggin' it out and stoppin' the infection. They were able to save the mare's life but it was touch and go for a while."

"How can these people sleep at night, Old Timer, these

trainers like Sammy Lee and Ellis and the rest of them? Don't they have a conscience? Don't they understand what they're doing is wrong?"

"That's a tough one, Junior. I think I told you before, I believe some of them are just plain mean and it doesn't bother them at all to torture animals. The others must rationalize it somehow. I'm sure greed plays a big part in it all. But I don't even pretend to understand the human mind, Son. Some of the horses I've talked to say that these people lie to themselves first. I guess they tell themselves that all these chemicals and gimmicks and devices are just part of trainin', that everybody does it, that they're doin' nothin' wrong. Once they start believin' themselves, it's easier for them to lie to others. When they get away with that, it becomes easier to believe their own lies, and so on. It's a vicious cycle. Pretty soon they have no idea what is really right or wrong anymore. Some of these owners and trainers that torture horses like you for personal gain, they go to church every Sunday. They profess to know and worship the Creator and to love and respect His creations. The whole while they're sittin' in that pew they've got horses at home down and moanin' in their stalls."

"A couple of the shows I was at, Old Timer, one of the trainers said a prayer over the loud speaker before the classes started. I remember thinkin' 'say a prayer for me while you're at it.'"

"Like I said, Junior, it's a tough one. Humans are hard to figure. They don't have horse sense."

"You said that you and Ellis Walsh go way back. What do you mean by that, Old Timer?"

"Well, he started me. Ellis and his helpers were the first to ride me back when I was not much older than you, Junior."

"Did they put you through the kind of hell that I'm going through, all these chemicals and things?"

"Well, not exactly. See, back then they mostly used just the oil of mustard. They hadn't come up with all this other stuff, yet.

Guess I got lucky. I was rescued early on and taken to California."

"You lived in California, Old Timer?"

"Of course I lived in California. That's where I did all my showin'. By the time I was moved back here, I was pretty much retired."

"Did you like it out there in California?"

"Sure I did, Junior. At first I missed my friends, familiar surroundings, and all that, you know. But I made some great friends out there and I was with one of the greatest Walking Horse trainers of all time."

"You're telling me you liked your trainer?"

"All the horses did, Junior, liked him and respected him to no end. The man became kind of a legend in the horse world because of the way he treated his animals. You have to earn respect, Junior – you know that – and earn the right to keep it."

"Didn't he sore you?"

"Not a once. He was totally against it. He worked us hard, don't get me wrong, especially comin' up to a show. But it was honest work, no painful chemicals, no nails in the quick, no ball bearings in the frog. Why, we didn't even show with chains for most of that time when everyone else was. When I first started we were shown with leather bell-boots on. They were actually designed to protect a horse if you over stepped too much and caught a quarter, or stepped on a front foot with a hind. There came a time when they changed the rules and people started showin' with chains on their horses, but not my trainer. He hated the idea."

"Who was this man, Old Timer?"

"His name was Royal Riggins and he was the best."

"You think he's still around, still training?"

"To be honest, Junior, I really don't know. I wish I did, though. It would be kinda nice to see him again before its time for me to cross that river.

"Cross what river?"

"I'm talkin' about that Great River that runs between this world and the next, Son. We've all got to cross it someday, and I've been feelin' it in my bones lately that my time might not be too far off. You know, I'm gettin' awful darn old for a horse. An old broken down gelding like me, that's seen pretty much all he wants to see of this world, you start to kinda look forward to crossin' over, Junior."

"You're not afraid?"

"Far from it, Son. Why should I be afraid? Horses like me and you got nothin' to worry about in the next world 'cept maybe gettin' too fat on that permanent pasture I hear runs as far as the eye can see. My mama told me a long time ago that the more trials and tribulations we are forced to endure here in this world, the easier we're likely gonna have it in the next. She used to say, 'Always hold your head up, Son, no matter what. Be strong and remember that if a man or a woman ever does you wrong, they will pay a price, while peace will be your reward.' She drilled that into me to no end. I guess 'cause she was so worried about the sorin' practices that were takin' over by then. I got lucky, Junior. I've had a good life."

"So you weren't with Ellis Walsh very long?"

"No, Royal Riggins came to our barn the year The Senator won the Grand Championship. I guess ol' Roy thought I had potential. Either that, or they were sellin' me real cheap. Anyways, I was shipped to California right after the Celebration that year. That was the year ol' Socks became a California resident."

"Socks?"

"Yeah, that's what they called me back then, before I got so old."

"You said before that I reminded you of someone, of a horse you knew once, a horse named Chief. Did you know him in California or back here?"

"You do remind me of ol' Chief. Yessir, you sure do."

"Well, was it here or in California, Old Timer, or should I say Old Socks?"

"Now, no need to get snippety, young Junior. Hold your vittles. What's got you so interested in ol' Chief, anyways? You heard stories about him?"

"I just might know something. But I want to make sure we're talking about the same horse. So, why don't you tell me about the Chief you know, or knew, then I'll tell you about the Chief I know."

"All right, all right. Well, like I said, I was moved to California and trained and shown out there by Royal Riggins. Sometime in the early 1970's, a big, strong, bay colt from Washington State was brought in for trainin'. He was three years old and had never been ridden. He acted like he'd never even been in a barn before. It took several men to push and pull him into his stall. I found out later that, sure enough, he never had been in a real barn except once in all his three years of life. Chief had pretty much been allowed to roam free up until then when his owners decided to send him to our barn."

"He was a wild horse then, Old Timer?"

"Well, I guess you could say that. He said he'd been caught up a couple times to get his hooves trimmed and get some shots but that was about it. His wild instincts were pretty well developed. It's a good thing his owners sent him to Royal Riggins instead of one of these rough, abusive, short-cut takin' trainers I've seen. He might have killed somebody. Royal was a man a horse could trust. He was honest. He wasn't always tryin' to trick you or hurt you. As it turned out, Chief learned faster than anybody.

"I heard Roy tell someone he actually preferred to start a colt like Chief that hadn't been spoiled by anyone. He figured if a horse didn't know anything about humans then he didn't know anything bad. His mind was a clean slate, his experience a blank canvas, and Roy could use his own natural talent and instincts to paint that canvas in the right way."

"If he was afraid of the barn, wasn't he afraid of people too?"

"Sure he was, Junior. But like I said, Royal Riggins was a man a horse could trust. And Chief needed to trust someone. He was out of his element. He was scared, away from the herd. It wasn't long before he was doin' whatever Roy asked him to. He learned fast but that wildness was always just under the surface, just under control. Roy said that's what made him such a great show horse, that wild spirit inside him.

"Chief was talented too. I mean he had a real natural, beautiful walk. Royal Riggins knew how to develop that talent. Not the way Sammy and them are treatin' you, Junior. He took his time. Roy trained Chief the old fashioned way, just like he'd learned from ol' Winston Wiser and S.W. Beech. Chief had a great natural stride with his hind legs kinda like yours truly, if I do say so, myself. He didn't have a tremendous headshake, nothin' exaggerated like you see today. He just nodded along real natural like. His front end wasn't great at first but it developed over the years, until he won Championships at Del Mar, Santa Barbara, Monterey, and elsewhere.

"Chief didn't really peak until he was five years old. That was the year he started winnin' everything. He was on the covers of magazines. Why, some enterprisin' individual even sketched an image copied from an action photo of Chief and put it on some tee shirts and sold a bundle of 'em. 'Course, they erased the rider off the horse for this endeavor and ol' Roy really got a kick out of that, Junior. He figured Chief was the one belonged on a tee shirt anyway, said he was more famous and better lookin' than his trainer any day.

"What was so amazin' about all of Chief's success, or any of us for that matter, was that we weren't sore. Here it was the middle 1970's heading into the last half of the decade, and we were still winnin' a lot and none of us sore. Chief, and some of the others, had never even seen a drop of mustard oil, or diesel fuel, or kerosene, or any of that stuff. They didn't know what it felt like 'cause they'd been started by Royal Riggins.

"Well, Junior, it was toward the end of the 70's that was really the end of an era for the Tennessee Walking Horse – in California, anyway. That's when the bad guys really took over.

"There'd been a lot of rule changes. The DQP's were now inspectin' the shows, in a joint effort by the Department of Agriculture and the Walking Horse industry. Talk about the fox guardin' the chicken coop! Anyone that was around then can tell you, that was the beginning of the end. The minute they took the authority and responsibility of inspectin' horses away from the horse show veterinarians and the American Horse Show Association, it was all down hill from there.

"Like I told you, they started showin' horses with chains instead of bell boots. The sore horse trainers were gettin' real inventive, comin' up with a lot of new ways to 'fix' their horses. Sure, they had 'government' inspectors, but they had their own people right in there with them to tip them off, to help 'em pass, Junior. The Horse Protection Act hardly even slowed them down. I suppose in a way, it even helped motivate the bad guys to find alternative methods of soring.

"We held on as long as we could, showin' clean. It just became harder and harder to beat the sore ones. They moved me down to the show pleasure division, but even those classes were bein' infiltrated. This was a real tough time for all of us. You could feel the tension buildin'. Royal Riggins' horses still won more classes than anybody else, but it was gettin' harder and harder to win.

It got to the point where a lot of times, his horses would be the only ones in the class that had not been chemically or mechaically altered in some way.

"Roy had made a decision long ago about sorin' horses and he was not about to change his mind. He overheard some Walking Horse people talkin' one day about how you could get through these new inspections if you just didn't over do it. They were sayin' everybody uses chemicals, you just have to be careful not to make your horse 'too sore', a 'bad image'. One of the people in the conversation, in fact, the person who made that statement, was a DQP inspector. Well, Roy couldn't let that pass. He was furious. He told them that as far as he was concerned, bein' a little bit sore was like bein' a little bit pregnant. Either you is or you ain't and that's it. When you're hot, you're hot. He even wrote a song about that. Most of these people, behind his back, accused Roy of sorin' his horses, too. How else could he do so much winnin'? That's how ignorant they were.

"They thought for sure that horses like Lacey and Chief and myself must be fixed somehow to be doin' what we were doin'. Their mentality just shows you how ingrained this sore train of thought, this method of trainin' horses was even back then, Junior, over twenty years ago. Just imagine how locked in it is now. This industry has been abusing animals since the middle 1950's. Why, the current generation of owners and trainers don't even have a memory of the Walking Horse business without soring. It is totally accepted. It's part of life. It's the way things are done. Just like cleanin' stalls or polishing tack, it's part of the routine."

"But what about Chief, did they put him down in the pleasure horse division, too?"

"No, Junior, he was too good for that. Like I said, he was still winnin' most of the time. We were still hangin' on, barely. When we got beat, it was usually by a sore horse. I guess that's what got to ol' Roy the most. He didn't mind gettin' beat fair and square. That's what showing is all about. But when your competition is cheatin' all the time and that's the only way they can beat you, it gets real hard to take for someone as competitive as he was."

"I bet ol' Chief didn't like getting beat by those sore horses either."

"He sure didn't. Chief was a proud horse and he had never been sored. What was bein' done to some of those horses was especially appalling to him. He felt sorry for those poor animals. But he also got mad. He couldn't understand why they didn't fight back more. Lacey and I tried to tell him it's just not that easy, 'cause we'd both been sored some early on before we came to Royal Riggins' barn. Well, Chief was stubborn and he'd grown up wild. He was his own horse. I'm surprised he didn't get into more trouble than he did."

THIRTEEN

"**H**e got in trouble with Mr. Riggins, Old Timer?"

"Not serious trouble. You know how in every group of horses it always seems like there's at least one horse that's good at gettin' out? Most every barn or pasture has one, some mare or gelding, or some stallion that's always gettin' a stall door open or openin' a gate. Well, in our barn Chief was that horse. He could open or untie most anything. He got out one night and opened one of the feed bins. I don't know how he did it but he's lucky he didn't founder himself. Another time he just went a visitin' once he got out of his stall. He went 'round to all the ladies in the barn to pay his respects, I suppose. He darned near got Miss Classy's door open and I think she was kinda hopin' he would for some reason.

"When we went to horse shows, the humans would always rig up a little somethin' extra on Chief's stall door to keep him in. They'd put a snap on the latch or run some balin' wire through it. If I happened to be stabled close enough to him I would hear him messin' with things all night long. Kept me up till I got used to it. He did get out at The Forum one time, but a friend of Roy's

recognized him and brought him back to us. Chief said he did it
'cause he was restless. Guess it had to do with the way he was
brought up, so wild and all. He just had a restless nature. He told
me he really enjoyed our company. It wasn't that. And he knew he
didn't want any other trainer besides Royal Riggins. Nevertheless,
well, one day Junior, that's exactly what happened."

"What happened? You all got a new trainer?"

"Not all at once Son, but eventually that's what happened. I
told you how ol' Roy was gettin' so fed up with the way the
Walking Horse business was goin'? He saw that we couldn't keep
beatin' the sore horses forever. Their methods were gettin' more
sophisticated, and more severe. The performance gait was
changing, gettin' out of hand. It was gettin' to where a sound horse
could not perform the desired gait. There was no way. Well, one
day I guess he'd just had enough. He decided to quit, to retire from
training. Let me tell you, Junior, that was a sad, sad day for the
Walking Horse world."

"So, what happened to all of you? Where'd you all go?"

"I was lucky. I'd already been showin' in pleasure classes by
then and for a time after Roy closed the barn, my owners took me
home and just rode me on the trails around their ranch. They had
a nice little place outside of San Diego, a little six-stall barn with
four horses. Ol' Roy even came down and rode me a few times
before Mrs. Armistead bought me and brought me back here. I got
the feelin' he really missed ridin' me, or any horse, to be honest
with you. The man was too young to retire from somethin' he
loved so much. Anyway, like I said, I was brought here for the
Missus to ride around once in a while. My showin' days are over,
thank goodness, so I don't have to go through any of the torment
that you go through."

"But what about Chief? What happened to him? Where did he
go?"

"That's the sad part Junior. Chief wasn't as lucky as I was, not by a long shot. Miss Lacey was bought by the Mussleman family and shown for another year or so before she started raisin' babies. Baldy's owners took him home and stood him as a breeding stallion. He thought he'd died and gone to heaven. Heard he's thrown some pretty nice colts, too. But Chief got the rough end of the stick, Junior. He sure did.

"Shortly before Royal Riggins retired, Chief was sold to people by the name of Olden, or Oldham. I think it was Oldham. These folks were new to show horses, Junior. In fact, Chief was the first show horse they ever owned. They didn't know all the history like I been tellin' you. They liked Chief 'cause he won. They weren't about to let one trainer's early retirement get in the way of some more blue ribbons. Even though they'd heard Roy preach many a time on the evils of sorin' and the virtues of doin' things right, they'd also heard people say ol' Roy was old-fashioned and livin' in the past. They'd started listenin' to the wrong crowd even before Roy's retirement. When he closed up shop, they wasted no time in takin' poor Chief over to Paul Chambers' stable.

"Chambers is a buddy and a contemporary of Sammy Belford's. They both learned a lot from Leonard Rust and Ellis Walsh. Just like the rest of the new breed of trainers, Paul Chambers would stop at nothin' to win, Junior. He was thrilled to get a hold of ol' Chief. He was tired of bein' beat by him. He'd had his eye on Chief for years. He figured that if Roy Riggins was sorin' the horse, he wasn't doin' enough of it. And that he, Paul Chambers, could really fix him up right if he ever got a hold of him. Now remember, Junior, Chief had never been sored, not once. He'd had one trainer his whole life, and that was Royal Riggins."

"Sounds like he was a lucky horse, Old Timer."

"Up to this point Junior, up to this point he was. That changed the minute he was put in that trailer and hauled over to Paul Chambers' place. Chambers couldn't wait to get on him. So, they got Chief out, saddled him up, slapped on some mustard oil and whatever else and a pair of heavy chains on his legs, and off they went. Off he went, I should say. I heard ol' Chief felt that fire on his legs for the first time and he balked and reared and pawed the air. Paul Chambers slid right off his back.

"Now, Chambers is a wiry little guy and he wasn't hurt seriously. But his ego was heavily bruised and he planned to take it out on Chief. With his helpers holdin' the horse, the trainer slowly got back on. He had one of them lead Chief by the bridle down the barn aisle to make sure he didn't rear. When he felt confident enough he told the man to release his hold and turn him loose. Chief took exactly two steps and up he went. Paul Chambers was prepared, or thought he was, with the butt end of a ridin' crop in his right hand. He smacked Chief on top of the head, and the horse came down but immediately bucked, sendin' his rider into the air and quickly, and painfully, to the ground.

"The assistant was quick enough to grab the reins and had a hold of the horse when Chambers got to his feet. The trainer commenced to whippin' and cussin' and tryin' to kick ol' Chief and the helper couldn't hold him. Chief broke free and was runnin' loose and mad and scared and big and strong. The barn doors were closed, so he couldn't run outside. The humans found safety in a stall or behind the door of the tack room. Paul Chambers grabbed his long lashed bullwhip and furiously stomped toward the end of the barn where Chief had stopped, snortin' and shakin' in a corner.

"What happened next put a stamp on Chief for the rest of his life, left a mark on Chambers, too, but in a more physical way. Before he got close enough to Chief to reach him with the whip, the trainer stopped and glared at him for a moment then cracked the big whip. He had misread the rage in the big stallion's eyes. He thought he saw fear and uncertainty, which I'm sure were there. What he didn't see was the anger and defiance, and the pure strength of the horse's soul.

"The sound of the whip was still hangin' in the air when Chief charged. He was on the man so fast he didn't even see him comin'. Chief fell on top of him, fell to his knees. One knee pinned Chambers to the ground, the weight of the horse on the man's broken leg. Then, Chief did the strangest thing. He bit the trainer's arm. The horses that saw it couldn't believe their eyes. I heard ol' Chief just sat there on his knees with the man's arm in his mouth, chewin' it like a dog on a bone.

"Well, the other men came and pulled the horse off of their boss and put him in his stall where he got the beatin' of his life. They gave him some drugs and poured a bunch of diesel fuel, and kerosene, and whatever else on his legs before wrappin' them in plastic. For the next several days and weeks, Chief was beaten and drugged and sored to no end. These men intended to beat him into submission, Junior, to break his spirit. But like I said, Chief was a big, strong, full-grown stallion with an endless spirit. He would not submit easily. He was very stubborn and that made it hard on him.

"Day after day, they worked on him. When they thought he was ready, they put the saddle on him and the assistant trainer, Danny, rode him in the barn aisle. Chief wasn't the same horse he'd been the last time they rode him, but he wasn't completely beaten down, either. He moved hesitantly, kinda jerky, like he didn't know what to do. These people didn't know what to think of him, a full-grown show horse who's been winnin' a lot, actin' like he's never been sored before. Well, they got two passes out of him before Chief had had enough. He stopped and reared and pawed the air with this Danny huggin' his neck. His rider was still mounted when Chief came down and stood on all fours.

"Danny jerked him around and dug in his spurs. Chief went up again, twistin' this time and walkin' a few steps on his hind legs. His rider couldn't hold on and Chief broke free to the corner of the barn. Once they got a hold of him they beat him again, then rode him a few more passes, quittin' before he could throw another fit.

"They repeated this sort of outing every three or four days with lots of sorin' and druggin' in between. It began to look like these men were gettin' the better of the proud bay stallion."

"I know the feeling, Old Timer."

"I know you do Junior, and I think it's important for you to know Chief's story."

"Yeah, me too."

"Well, like I said, it was startin' to look like they were gettin' the better of him but they still didn't trust him completely. He was rearin' and buckin' less but he would still surprise them once in a while. The stable boys couldn't clean his stall without takin' him out first. Sometimes Chief was already out of his stall when they got there in the mornin'. Remember, I told you how good he was with latches and such. Well, even as drugged and as sore and as beat as he was, the old Chief would still shine through from time to time.

"When these men took him out of his stall to clean it, they usually put him in a small round, wooden pen behind the barn while they did their work. Chief enjoyed this time outside, Junior. I think it kinda recharged him to feel the sun on his back and the wind in his mane. He remembered his early days in the Washington apple country, runnin' free through the lush green pasture. He came out of his tortured haze long enough one day to break some of the one-by-six planks of the pen, which of course, brought more punishment upon him.

"The next time they cleaned his stall, which was several days later, the planks in the round pen had still not been repaired. Beside the pen, just a few yards away, was an area where Chambers' young daughter had kept her 4-H calf penned up for a time. The men had run electric 'hot' wire through some stakes in the ground, and this had been enough to keep the Angus heifer from wanderin'.

"Now, Junior, everybody knows that horses and hot wire

don't always mix well. I don't know if you've ever been around it or not, but it is scary stuff. We all know that cows aren't as smart as horses, of course. But when it comes to dealin' with the personality of somethin' like hot wire, they're a lot better suited to it than we are, especially when you're talkin' about a high-strung stallion like ol' Chief. Chief had never seen electric wire before. He didn't know what it was. Nevertheless, that's where these men put him, in that little wire enclosure. Then they turned on the juice. I guess they had no love lost for the big, bay pain in the butt, and if he got hurt, hey, maybe it would teach him a lesson. Besides, he was insured, right?"

"Did he escape, Old Timer? Did he run away from there somehow?"

"The answer to that is, yes. He did ultimately escape. But not in the way you're thinkin'. At first, Chief was only interested in what available grass he could nibble on. He had been off his feed lately due to all the drugs and chemicals and the abuse he was gettin'. His memory of the fresh green pasture grass of his youth, although faded, was far better than the slim pickin's out behind the barn there in the Chino Hills, but he kept searchin'. The morning sun glanced off the thin wire that surrounded him and he realized that was all that was holdin' him. There was no real fence, no boards, no wall, just that thin shiny, pulsating wire.

"Now, Junior, I want you to remember that Chief is really not himself at this point. He's not the same bright, brave, invincible stallion he had once been. His senses are dulled, his spirit almost broken. The men had been givin' him high doses of anti-inflammatories and sedatives, then to perk him up they gave him stimulants. So, like I said Chief was not himself."

"Believe me, I know how he was feeling."

"I know you do, Junior. Well, Chief was tryin' to reach a little patch of green grass outside the area he was confined to that day. He stretched his head underneath the hot wire and got a couple good bites when a cat ran by and startled him. He raised his head up so quickly he forgot about the wire and hit it hard. It shocked him and kept shockin' him. He didn't understand what was happening. He panicked. He kept pullin' back and turnin' and twistin', and somehow the wire wrapped around his throat. The stakes pulled out of the ground. The wire was still hot, the pulsating shock hittin' Chief every other second. The more he fought it and tried to get away, the more the wire twisted around his neck. Some of it wrapped around his feet and he fell to the ground. He kept tryin' to kick it off, but all that did was pull the wire tighter around his neck. Eventually, he stopped kickin' and just lay still, an occasional involuntary jerk the only sign of life from the big stallion. The cat saw the whole thing. When all movement ceased, she was the first one to know that the horse the humans said was so mean, would be mean no longer."

"Oh, Old Timer, what a way to die. Didn't anybody hear Chief struggling besides the cat?"

"I guess not, Junior, or if they did they didn't care."

"That is so sad."

"Tell me about it. That big horse was my friend and I can't tell that story without the tears wellin' up, Son. But ol' Chief saw an end to his torment that day. Legend has it, at least accordin' to some, that Chief knew exactly what he was doin'. That he was not goin' to let those men abuse him anymore. They say his will was so strong against it and so bent on freedom he saw that there wire was his ticket out and he took it. I've heard some horses even say they have seen him at night, runnin' free like he just got out of his stall. Some say they have heard him callin' to them, seen him in their dreams."

"I never told you before, Old Timer, but I've been seeing Chief in my dreams for some time now. I've been seeing him more and more often, him and other horses from the past. Sometimes I'm not even sure it is a dream."

"Does he talk to you Junior? In your dreams, I mean. Does Chief talk to you?"

"Yes, he talks to me. He helps me out of situations. He gives me advice."

"He gives you advice?"

"I know it sounds crazy, Old Timer. Chief is just as real to me as you are. He has become a close friend and confidant. It's like he understands what I'm going through and he wants to help, he and the others."

"I don't think it sounds crazy at all, Junior. I have dreams all the time where I'm runnin' into my old friends. The older I get the more often I have 'em. I just have never run across ol' Chief yet, like you have."

"Well, whenever I see him it's like he's on a mission. He's always trying to tell me something, to help me out."

"That makes sense 'cause the other horses that have told me about seein' Chief, they said the same thing. That's part of the legend. It's the horses that are bein' hurt the most, that are sufferin' the most abuse, who are most likely to get a visit from the big bay's spirit. I guess he figures I've got it too easy to come see me. He wants to comfort horses like you, Junior, who really need it. I haven't been sored in years. I'm just sittin' around tellin' stories and waitin' to die."

"Well, I don't know about the others, but as for myself, I welcome his presence. Chief and the other horses do comfort me. I'm still afraid of those dreams of battlefields and soldiers, of the violence in them. But I guess I've come to realize that I need the escape from reality, the change of scene the dreams bring me, and that I've got plenty of violence, and evil, here in my own life. Sometimes, Old Timer, it just all runs together. The chemicals, the soring, the drugs, the war, the horse shows, the battles, the beatings, the spirit-horses, you and the horses here in the barn, the blue devil-soldiers, the evil trainers – it's all a part of my experience."

"I know what you're sayin', Junior. Dreams can be very real sometimes and very informative. What is it that Chief is tryin' to tell you in these dreams? Do you know?"

"First of all, Chief is always the one that unties me and the other horses, frees us from the picket line or the trees where we're being held."

"That sounds like Chief all right. Then what?"

"Then, once we're all loose, we sneak off through the woods until we get to the road that leads to the river."

"The river?"

"Yeah, that's how most all the dreams end – we're running down that road or across a field towards the river. The devil-soldiers that look like Sammy, Jeremy, and William are chasing us, and Traveler, and Chief, and sometimes Gray John, are saying, 'go to the river, swim to the other side, that's where you'll be safe.'"

"Your dreams always end like this, Junior?"

"Most always. What do you think it means?"

"Well, I think it sounds important, that's for sure! If most of your dreams are endin' the same way, they are most likely tryin' to tell you somethin'. Do you ever make it to the river?"

"No, not yet. We get awful close sometimes and it looks like we're gonna make it, then I wake up, Old Timer. Or should I call you Socks? I keep forgetting I know your real name now."

"Oh, it's been so long since anybody called me that, I'm just used to Old Timer now, Junior. So, you never quite make it to the river, huh? What's it like, can you tell? Is it a big river?"

"I'm not sure. Not real big, I guess. I know one thing, though, the closer I get to that river, the better I feel. The pain in my legs starts going away. I feel more relaxed. I want to jump in the water. I want to swim across. I feel drawn to it. Chief and them don't have to urge me on at that point. It's like the river is calling me to it, Old Timer."

Sammy Lee Belford was worried about his two-year old stallion contender. Junior had been acting listless lately and it was getting close to the big show. The Celebration was just three weeks away. He was also concerned about the all too-apparent scaring on Junior's legs. The trainer and his assistants had tried to keep the scarring to a minimum, but even with today's techniques, scarring did occur. It looked like he needed another sloughing off, another acid treatment.

So, once again, Junior was subjected to one of the most painful ordeals these horses go through. The salicylic acid was applied to his lower legs, the legs were wrapped and he was returned to his stall to endure the days of excruciating pain that follows.

It was during this time that Junior experienced his most vivid dream ever. He was back in the woods with the smell and the tension of war surrounding him. He was afraid. He was alone and the sounds of the battle were becoming more and more distant. He looked and listened for his friends, but no one was around. His feet were bleeding and hurting badly. He had to lie down, even though it could be dangerous. Keeping in sight of the narrow dirt road, which could bring either friend or foe, he hid himself behind a clump of green nettles and pokeweed, and waited.

A column of Blue soldiers galloped down the road in not so orderly fashion. They didn't see the young bay stallion hiding in the weeds, but not long after these passed, more riders approached. Junior couldn't tell if they wore blue or gray. As he tried to get a better look, he unintentionally shook the bushes he was lying against. This caught the attention of one of the front riders. The man raised his hand and the riders halted with their weapons at ready.

"Who goes there?" said the tall Gray soldier.

Junior didn't answer, but his tail, which had caught on

a bramble, let them know he was still there. The tall man dismounted and approached the bushes with gun in hand. When he saw Junior he shook his head and smiled. His smile quickly disappeared when he saw the colt's legs.

"Johnson, Millett, give me a hand over here!"

The men treated Junior's wounds as best they could and wrapped his legs in cloth from an old shirt. Junior was standing now and feeling better.

"What we gonna do with him, Colonel Riggins? He's awful beat up."

"I don't know, Johnson. I know he's been hurt pretty bad but he sure is a nice looking colt, young and strong, smart looking. Make somebody a mighty good mount once he's healed up."

Just then a shot rang out, then a volley. The man called Johnson fell to the ground dead, a dark red hole in his forehead. Colonel Riggins yelled to his men: "Take to the woods and scatter! Reconvene at the aforementioned!"

Then he swung himself onto Junior's back and rode him across the road into the woods. Bullets were flying everywhere. Junior could hear them buzz by his head. Chips of bark stung his face as the mini-balls hit nearby trees. His feet didn't hurt anymore and the rider on his back was practically motionless as he hugged the horse's neck and guided him through the thick brush and trees.

The next thing Junior knew, they were waiting out a storm in an old barn with a leaky roof. Colonel Riggins was combing the mane of a young black gelding that had a white snip on his nose and two white hind socks.

"Now, Socks," the colonel was saying, "I want you to help me take care of this new recruit of ours. He seems kind of green. I know you're old beyond your years so help me show him the ropes, all right?"

"I think he meant 'wise beyond my years'. Don't you,

Junior?"

"I think they go hand in hand, Old Timer, whatever he meant."

All of a sudden, a flash of white light lit up the whole barn. Shortly after a very loud thunderclap, Junior heard the unmistakable crackle of hay and wood burning. The rain had stopped. He could smell the awful smoke and he wanted to bolt. He was in a stall that was just like his stall at Sammy Belford's stable and Old Timer was next to him. They were both trapped in their stalls. Junior reared and pawed at the door, but it wouldn't budge. He began to run around his stall in a panic. Old Timer was panicky, too, though he just stood there, trying to remember something.

"Wiggle the door, Socks. Use your head, it slides, remember. Put your nose up against it and slide it to the right. I undid your latch from out here." It was Chief, and he was standing in the barn aisle outside their stalls giving his instructions to Socks.

"Remember how I used to do it? Use your nose and slide it." Socks was trying. Though he kept losing his grip, he was moving the door a couple inches at a time. Soon it was open far enough for him to stick his head through. He pushed it the rest of the way with his neck, then rushed out of the stall to stand next to his old friend Chief.

"Okay, now I'm going to show you how to undo the latches, Socks. Watch closely, then do what I do. Use your lips on these, your teeth if you can. Get a hold of it like it's a carrot, then up and back. Got it? Up and back, push it back and it will stay there, Socks. We don't have much time. I'm going to go down one side and you go down the other. Undo all the latches you can. Start with Junior's here, then, slide the door with your head, like you did yours. I know you can do it. I'm counting on you."

Junior didn't really understand all that was going on between Chief and Socks. He was jumping around his stall, panicking, barely aware that his hero and mentor, Chief was even there.

Socks, or Old Timer, was not overtaken by panic. Chief had given him a job to do and he was doing his level best to do it. He knew it was important and that time was of the essence. He remained calm, concentrating on his work. He got Junior's door open after fumbling ineptly with the latch for what seemed like a long time. The next one was easier and so was the next until he got quite good at it. The problem was none of the horses would come out of their stalls. Their doors were wide open and they just stood there. Some of them came out, only to run back into the security of their stall at the sight of the flames and the smoke that were everywhere by now.

Junior was one of those who initially, after Old Timer opened his door, ran out then ran back in. Too scared to move.

"Come with us! Follow me, Junior!"

Junior knew that voice. It was Traveler. Gray John, Merry Go Boy, Roan Allen, and Merry Legs all suddenly appeared. Then, they were all outside the barn, away from the fire, and running down that familiar road.

FOURTEEN

Old Timer let out a loud welcome whinny when he heard the men talking as they entered the barn. Junior heard him, but he wasn't sure if it was real or in his dream. He just lay there and moaned in his third day of salicylic acid hell.

"I heard that Mrs. Armistead bought Socks and brought him back here. So, I thought I'd come say hello to the old fella. I hope you don't mind. How's he doing?"

"Old Socks? He's doing great. He's got it pretty easy these days. Too old to be ridden, so he just eats and sleeps. We turn him out once in a while when the weather's good. Are you still ridin' some?"

"Once in a while, when I feel up to it."

"You come back here for the Celebration, Roy?"

"Actually, my son Rick just bought a place not too far from here and we're out visiting him. To be honest with you, things have changed so much that I don't have much desire to see the show."

"I heard Ricky got in the music business in Nashville."

"Yeah, he's had some luck with some of his songs, had a few hits."

"Is that right?"

"Hey, Sammy, you've got a phone call. It's Mr. Cherry," Jeremy yelled from down the barn.

"You'll have to excuse me, Roy. Socks' stall is the last one on your left, right down there."

Old Timer let out another call to his old trainer. He would recognize that voice anywhere, even after all these years. How had he found him?

"Hello, Socks, old boy." Royal Riggins stood outside the stall for a moment, then opened the door to get a better look at his old friend. He stepped in the stall and held out his hand for Socks to smell, then rubbed the horse's neck and scratched the side of his head just like he used to. Socks responded with a short, low nicker of appreciation.

"It's been a long time, ol' Son. We sure had some good times didn't we, boy? Before this business got so crazy. We were lucky, I guess, that we came along when we did, you and I." Roy ran his horseman's hand and practiced eye down the old horse's legs and looked him over closely.

"Looks like you're doing pretty good, Old Timer, considering. A little grayer than you used to be, but so am I. Seeing you makes me want to grab a saddle and bridle and jump on your back one more time, but I'm afraid that might be a little too much for both of us."

Old Timer was elated to see this man he thought about so much. He couldn't believe it. Roy was actually here. He wanted to show him off to Junior. "See, Junior, this is the famous Royal Riggins, trainer extraordinaire. The man who trained and showed Tennessee Walking Horses without hurtin' them." But Junior was still down, in severe pain from the sloughing off process. Socks really wanted Roy to meet Junior. As the old man stepped back briefly from the old horse, Old Timer walked over to the wall he shared with Junior and looked pitifully down on his young friend. He looked back at Royal, then at Junior again. The man thought this was peculiar behavior for the old horse and wondered what he was looking at in the next stall. He walked over and saw Junior lying there and heard him moan. He knew immediately the horse was in pain.

"It's his legs, isn't it old boy, some darn chemical they've put on him. And he's not the only one. When I walked in this barn I noticed all the other horses were lying down, too. It's not right. Ricky warned me about this. That's why he didn't come – he knew he'd get too upset. He wanted to see you, Socks, but just couldn't take walking in here and seeing all this and being cordial to Sammy Lee Belford. He still remembers how we think it was Sammy that sored you at Indio that time, still calls him Sammy the Snake. You know, Rick has offered to buy you several times, but the old lady won't sell. She says you've got a good home and you've been such a pleasure to her, she won't let you go."

Junior moaned again and Royal said to Old Timer, "I wish there was something I could do for that colt. I just hate that all this is going on, Socks, I really do. I know you do, too. Say, he kinda looks like ol' Chief, doesn't he?"

Just then, Sammy Lee walked up. "He's looking pretty good for an old fart, ain't he, Roy."

"Yeah, Socks is looking good, but this colt next to him sure isn't. What's wrong with him?" The older man asked, as if he didn't know.

"Now don't be getting uppity on me, Roy. You know there's things we got to do these days to get these horses ready to show."

"This colt looks like he's in a lot of pain right now."

"Like I said, don't be getting all high and mighty on me. This is my barn. I'm the trainer here. Competition's tough out there, Roy, and you have to get these horses right, to compete. You know that. I know you were always saying what we were doing was wrong. But you can't compete without it these days. It's just the way things are done now and it's none of your business, anyhow. I hear the government's gonna be at Shelbyville again this year but I'll be in compliance, don't you worry."

"You call this being in compliance?"

"Hey, this colt will be ready to show and he will pass. I guarantee it. We've got rules to go by. 'Course, it would be a lot easier if the USDA would leave us alone altogether. We might not have to worry about them much longer."

"What do you mean?"

"We're about to talk them into letting us police ourselves, completely, with no interference from anybody. We've been working on it for several years now, and it's looking like we're getting close. I think they're tired of messing with us, tired of spending the money. I think we've got them convinced we can take care of ourselves. It's just around the corner, no more government. That was Mr. Cherry on the phone, and he said things are looking real good right now in that department."

"I can't believe they would turn you guys loose like that."

"Come on, now, Roy. Have a little faith."

"Oh, I've got plenty of that, Belford. That's why I have to believe that someday this will all come to an end and your slimy, stinking ways of getting rich off the suffering of these poor animals will no longer be tolerated."

"All right, it's time for you to leave, old man. If you was younger I'd deck you first. Mrs. Armistead asked me to be nice to you, and I have. You've seen your old broken-down horse. Now you need to go."

Roy was thinking, "If I was a younger man it would be me doing the decking, not you, Sammy the Snake." Before he left, he gave Old Timer-Socks another little neck rub and said, "You know, old boy, we will meet again someday. But it won't be in this world. It will be up yonder, where this kind of evil won't stand. I just wish there was something I could do for your young friend here. He sure reminds me an awful lot of ol' Chief. You remember Chief don't you Socks? He found a way out of all this, not long after we closed the barn, from what I heard. Well, see you later, Socks."

The old man's eyes filled as he walked away from his old friend, happy to have seen him once again and so sad to have witnessed the suffering of the rest of the horses in the barn, especially the young bay colt. The image of Junior lying there moaning in pain would not easily leave his mind. How long will this go on, this torture of innocent animals? He was ashamed to say he had even been a Tennessee Walking Horse trainer. He had nothing in common with the people who could do this for a living.

Old Timer watched and listened as Royal Riggins left the barn. He heard a car start up and listened to the sound the tires made on the gravel drive as it faded in the distance. For a moment, when his old trainer was rubbing his neck and talking to him, he was taken back to his glory days in California. He remembered how it felt to have Roy in the saddle putting him through his paces, going to the horse shows, talking to Lacy and Midnight. He wished Roy had brought that old dog with him. Then he realized Midnight probably left this earth years ago. "Heck, he was old when I knew him," thought Old Timer. "Well, it won't be long 'fore I'll be joinin' him."

"Sure wish I could help you out somehow before I go, Junior."

"What are you talking about, Old Timer?"

"You awake Junior? I thought you were still plum out of it, off in that dream world of yours."

"No, I've been awake for a while, kinda drifting in and out, I guess. I thought I heard a man talking to you."

"You did. You did, indeed. That was Royal Riggins. I've told you about him, Junior."

"Royal Riggins, the trainer you're always raving about?"

"That's right, one and the same, right here in my stall. He came all the way from California just to see me, to pay his respects while we're both still walkin' this earth."

"He came all the way from California just to see you?"

"Well, he did say he was visitin' his son, Ricky, while he was here. Guess the boy bought hisself a farm down the road apiece. While you're awake, I want to tell you I had a dream last night. You were in it. You and Chief and a bunch of other horses I thought I knew."

"Tell me about it, Old Timer, because I had a dream with you in it."

"We were in a barn, a big barn like this, and it caught fire. Before it caught fire, Royal Riggins was there and he told me to take care of you, to watch over you 'cause you were young. In the dream I was young, too, just not as young as you, I guess."

"What happened, when it caught fire?"

"Well, Chief was there. He showed me how to open the doors of the stalls so that you and the other horses could get out, get away from the fire. I told you Chief was always good at gettin' in or out of stall doors and gates and things."

"Did you recognize some of the other horses, Old Timer?"

"I sure did. They were horses from the past, our ancestors."

"Old Timer, I had the same dream! And you were in it. You were in my dream and I was in yours. Don't you see? We had the same dream! We were there together. That means something, doesn't it?"

"That's strong, all right. Down right powerful meanin', I'd say. I'm gettin' one of my feelin's again, Junior, like something's gonna happen. Don't know if it's bad or good, but something's gonna happen real soon, to both of us."

"Your feelings? What's that? What do you mean?"

"I mean, somethin' big is gonna happen, Junior. I know a feelin' when I feel it, and this is a feelin'. Havin' the same dream, that didn't just happen for no reason. No, sir."

"What are you talking about, Old Timer? What's gonna happen?"

"I don't know exactly what it is that's gonna happen. I just know that it's gonna be big. It's gonna be real important to both of us. Gonna affect us, Junior, you and me."

"Well, let me know when it happens. I'm going to lay my head back down and try to take a nap. I wish they would bring me some water, Old Timer. I'm not sure I can stand up right now, but I sure am thirsty."

"I'm kinda wore out, myself. Feels like nap time to me, too. Maybe I'll have another dream."

That evening, William set up the new Accelerator filly with plenty of kerosene and collodion on her legs, then placed the containers back in the storage room. He did so in a rather detached state of mind. He had not been feeling well lately, and was having an increasing number of headaches and stomachaches. He had developed a curious skin rash and was beginning to wonder if any, or all, of the chemicals he handled each day could be the source of his problems.

Almost all of them emitted toxic fumes. Hadn't an oil of mustard spill caused the evacuation of an entire post office in Indiana? He'd seen it on the news and heard it from his friends. The liquid was being shipped from one Walking Horse trainer to another. The box containing the chemical was accidentally dropped, causing the spill, panic, and evacuation. A toxic cleanup crew, complete with space suits and gas masks, was dispatched to sterilize the situation. Constantly handling these chemicals could not be good for him.

His health concerns weighing on his mind, William didn't notice the cap to the kerosene can was askew and barely in place when he sat it on the shelf. He absent-mindedly placed the nearly empty container so that part of it was hanging over the edge. He also failed to notice that the sole of his boot missed his carelessly tossed, half-smoked cigarette by at least two inches.

Later that night, all the horses were either asleep or close to it and human activity was limited to the sound of William's television trying to drown out his mostly staccato snoring pattern. In the storage room, a rather anxiously maternal deer mouse was collecting nest material in the form of shredded pages from a discarded Voice of The Tennessee Walking Horse magazine.

She didn't notice that the loosely capped can of kerosene sat precariously on the edge of the shelf, or that the magazine she was so vigorously tugging at was partially pinned underneath this very can. Her activity was inching the can over the edge of the shelf, but that didn't bother her. The still-smoldering remains of a cigarette on the floor below caused her no concern. Her focus was on the procurement of paper for her nest. She ignored the "hazardous material" label on the container of collodion that warned of possible explosion and of the release of poisonous gases in the case of such an event. This industrious and purposeful little deer mouse had been scuttling in and around containers of kerosene, diesel fuel, mustard oil, collodion, salicylic acid, and the like for days now. She had no idea of the enormity of the chain of events she was about to set in motion.

The determined mother-to-be was almost finished with her nest and needed just one more bunch of paper to add to the pile, but the page was not tearing easily. She was down close to the binding of the magazine and it held at her first little tugs. She pulled harder, moving the part that was underneath the kerosene can ever so slightly, but moving it farther over the edge of the shelf. She wiggled around and gave it one more hard tug from the other direction. When the paper gave way, the mouse's momentum carried her backward into the hazardous container.

As it hit the floor, the can's lid flew off sending a small river of kerosene toward the awaiting glow of the cigarette. The river ignited, and the room was quickly engulfed in flames while the mouse escaped through a hole in the wall. Soon, the over heated container of collodion exploded loudly, awakening William, who ran to investigate. He grabbed a fire extinguisher when he saw smoke creeping out underneath the door to the storage room. As he opened the door, the toxicity of the gases overcame him and he fell choking and gasping to the floor.

The explosion also awakened Old Timer and Junior from their respective repose, although Junior remained on the floor of his stall.

"What was that, Old Timer?"

"I'm not sure, Son. But, it didn't sound good. I think I see smoke at the other end of the barn. Can you stand up?"

"I don't know. I can try."

"Just see if you can get up and on your feet in case we need to get out of here. I can definitely see smoke now, and flames. I wonder where William is?"

At that moment, the horses could hear smoke alarms going off, along with more explosions from the storage room. Mrs. Armistead had long ago equipped the barn with state of the art smoke and heat detectors along with an extensive sprinkler system. Such systems require maintenance, and that had not been a priority of Sammy Lee Belford's. The overhead sprinklers were activated. Junior and Old Timer were getting soaked, but only their side of the barn was being wet down. Regular maintenance would have discovered the badly corroded pipes in the middle of the barn, which were now keeping water from reaching the area where it was most needed. The flames spread quickly.

Without really thinking about what he was doing, Old Timer began rubbing his nose on the inside of his stall door, pushing it and moving his head from left to right. To his amazement the door was moving. It wasn't latched! Royal Riggins must have forgotten to latch it when he left earlier that day after visiting the old horse. What was this like? The dream, of course! The dream that both he and Junior had had the night before, this was it. The fire, the water, the open door, he had been through this all before. His door was now open enough for him to stick his head through. He pushed it the rest of the way open and stepped out into the aisle of the barn.

Once outside his own stall, the old horse continued to act as he had in his dream. He remembered how Chief had shown him to play with the latch on Junior's stall door until it opened. He took it in his mouth and jiggled it, fumbled with it with his lips, then his teeth. What was it Chief had told him? Up and back, that's it. Up and back.

While Old Timer was working on the latch, people were beginning to arrive. The activation of the sprinkler system, such as it was, had triggered alarms at the house and at the security company, who in turn had called the fire department. No one saw William lying on the floor inside the storage room, where the fire had started, as they began to open stall doors and remove the horses. The main concern was for the horses nearest the flames. No one noticed that Old Timer was already out and working furiously on Junior's door.

Up and back. He was trying but he kept losing his grip. The old horse's teeth were not what they once were. He knew how important this was. If he ever did anything in his life, he needed to do this. He thought he heard Chief standing behind him, urging him on. Junior was on his feet now and pushing on the door with his nose, pawing at it with his feet.

"Junior, stop it! I'm tryin' to do somethin' here. You're not makin' it any easier. Quit moving the door."

Junior heard but didn't listen, and kept nudging and kicking at the door. Old Timer didn't realize that Junior's actions were actually helping him. Eventually, he got it right and the latch pushed back.

Old Timer and Junior worked together on sliding the door open, and this was quickly accomplished. Junior ran out into the barn aisle to join his friend. The sights and smells and sounds of the fire, the men yelling, horses screaming, drove him right back in his stall.

"Come on Junior! Come back out of there, we've got to go!" Old Timer pleaded.

"Come on, Son. You know what you've got to do. We've practiced it a million times." It was Traveler talking, and beside him was Chief.

"You have got to get out of there and you've got to do it now! Understand? Run out the end of the barn with old Socks here. Chief and I will be with you shortly. We'll show you where to go. There's no need to be afraid. Don't we always rescue you? Don't we always take care of you? Well, this isn't any different, except that it's more important this time because it's real."

Junior wasn't sure any of this was real. It was so much like the dream he'd had last night. Here were Chief, Traveler, and other spirit horses he knew from his dreams, rescuing him from the brink of disaster once again. The fact that they'd been in similar situations before made it easier to trust these horses and to believe that what Traveler said was true. Junior bolted from the imagined safety of his own stall to join Old Timer, Traveler, Chief, and Gray John outside of the barn.

Once outside, he began to have his doubts again. Junior had rarely been outside of the barn, especially where they were now at the back of the barn. In front of them he saw the rows of four-plank wood fencing that made up the outside paddocks. Even though there was a good sized moon out – and some additional light from the fire – it was still the middle of the night, and fences, trees, horses, and outbuildings were mostly just shadows and indistinct shapes in the dark.

In this moment of uncertainty, Old Timer had a question for Junior:

"What is it that always happens at the end of your dreams? I remember you told me that they almost always end the same, with you and your friends runnin' for something."

"The river, Old Timer, we always run for the river."

"That's right, now I remember."

"But there's no river around here, is there?"

"Sure there is, Junior, out beyond the paddock area there, on the other side of the big pasture. The Duck River runs right along the back edge of this farm, on it's way to Shelbyville and Normandy Lake."

"How do you know all that?"

"'Cause, when I first moved here I was turned out most the time. I keep my eyes and ears open, you know. So I've got a pretty good idea of the layout of this place."

"Well, can we get to the river from here? It's pretty dark and it looks like there's an awful lot of fence between here and where you say the river runs. I've got half a mind to walk right back in that barn and lay down in my stall. My feet are hurting awful bad."

"If you went and did that, Junior, I would say you have half a mind. We can't just stand around here yappin'. Let's get movin' in the right direction, anyway." Old Timer pleaded.

"Follow me, Boys!" It was Traveler, and he was headed down the dirt road that ran between the wooden paddocks, toward the back pasture. Junior was still feeling uncertain and kept looking over his shoulder at the burning barn. Then – real or imagined – he thought he saw Sammy Lee and someone else run out of the barn in their direction. They were yelling something he could not understand. Sammy raised his right hand and was waving either a riding crop or a sword. Junior wasn't sure which it was in the poor light. He didn't feel like sticking around to find out and ran down the road with Traveler and the others. Old Timer ran along side him like he knew exactly where they were going.

FIFTEEN

"**R**emember, Junior, run to the river and swim to the other side. That's where you'll be safe." Traveler's commanding voice was unmistakable. Old Timer heard him, too. He saw him clearly in the moonlight, a proud, muscular Thoroughbred type, who was most likely a distant relative, or possibly even an ancestor of his and Junior's. As they progressed down the dirt road, Old Timer began to feel his age a bit. Junior, despite his cumbersome and weighty pads and shoes and the pain that each step brought him, was in great shape and some thirty years younger. Old Timer was unsure how long he could keep up. He knew it was important for them – for Junior at least – to reach the river that ran behind the farm. Traveler and Chief had made that clear, and Old Timer was going to do anything within his power to help his young friend.

He was breathing heavily now, after just this short run, and he wasn't at all sure he could make it to the water. Still, he knew he must not hinder his friend's attempt at reaching that goal. Old Timer remembered that, up ahead, there was a gate leading to the back pasture that they must enter before attaining the river. Was the gate open or closed? He couldn't tell from where he was. If it was closed, they would be trapped. How would they open it? Could Chief show him how to open it before their pursuers reached them? He doubted that. He saw it in the dim light. The gate was closed!

Old Timer was still running along side his friend, but tiring quickly. He wanted desperately to see Junior escape – if only briefly – from Sammy Lee, and Jeremy, and the daily torment he experienced. It was obvious that the spirit horses shared his desire. The closed gate would prevent this from happening. Or would it?

Junior didn't know about the gate. To him, the barrier was just one of many mysterious shadows in the dim light. He was more concerned about his old friend, who was obviously laboring from the exertion of their midnight run. So, he was taken by surprise when Old Timer, in a sudden burst of speed and adrenalin, passed him and took the lead in the race for the river.

The old horse even surprised himself a little bit with the sudden strength and daring of his move. Inspired by the presence of the likes of Traveler, Chief, and Gray John, he plowed full force into the wooden gate. He thought that if he hit it hard enough, it might crumble under his weight and open the way for them to escape to the open pasture, and the river beyond. He thought he remembered the gate being rather old and rickety when he had been turned out back here. He hoped it still was.

The pain on impact was more than the old horse had anticipated, but it didn't last long. He took the brunt of the hit with his chest, and as the top of the gate gave way, he fell forward, getting his front feet tangled in the boards at the bottom. The sheer weight of the horse combined with his speed demolished the wooden gate but he couldn't keep his feet. Old Timer's momentum carried his body forward, and as his knees and head hit the ground and tangled in the broken gate, his hind legs somersaulted over his body and snapped his spinal cord.

It happened so fast that Junior wasn't sure exactly what had happened. He had seen Old Timer go down but was running so fast he couldn't stop. He jumped over the tangled wreckage and into the open field beyond. When he was able to stop himself, he realized that his good friend was no longer with him. He had fallen down. He was hurt. Junior began to turn around and head back to the gate where Old Timer had fallen, when Chief and Traveler stopped him.

"There's nothing you can do, Junior, believe me. Socks will be just fine," said Chief.

"Remember the river. You're half way there. Straight ahead across this field is where you must go. Don't turn back now," the commanding voice of Traveler told him.

"But, what about Old Timer, he might be hurt. I can't just leave him."

"Don't worry about me, Junior. Let's go! Destiny awaits." His old friend had appeared as if from nowhere. Junior was so glad to see him that he didn't notice the still, lifeless body of a horse that lay back at the gate.

"Old Timer, are you all right? But, how did y..."

"Like I said, Junior, don't worry about me. We've got to get you to the river! Let's go!"

As Junior continued his run to the river he noticed how young and refreshed Old Timer looked. He made no comment and concentrated on the task at hand. As he and his friends got closer to the row of trees and brush that lined the river bank, Junior could smell the water and it seemed to breathe new life into him. His feet were still hurting, but not as much. The excitement of the fire, their escape, and the accompanying adrenalin rush, all helped his pain fade to the back of his mind. They were almost there. The smell of the river was strong now. Not much farther. What was this? Another fence?

Just when it seemed his goal was within reach, here was another obstacle. When Junior reached the fence, he ran alongside it to his right. After fifty feet or so, he stopped and turned, running along the fence in the opposite direction, constantly looking over it toward the river. He paced anxiously back and forth several times. He heard Traveler speaking to him.

"I've got to leave you now, Junior. Chief and John and I have work to do back at the barn. There are other horses who need help."

"But what about the fence? How do I get to the river?"

"Socks will show you. He will be your guide now. Listen to what he says, and remember, swim to the other side. You will be safe there. Goodbye." Junior watched as Traveler, Chief and Gray John ran back toward the burning barn. He was momentarily at a loss when Old Timer, who didn't seem so old anymore, beckoned him.

"This way, Junior. Come down this way, along the fence."

"I've already been down that way, it's no use." He went, in spite of his doubts in the direction his friend was indicating. Junior could almost hear the river calling him. As in his dreams, he felt an irresistible desire to jump in the water. He ran along the fence, bumping into it from time to time as if to see if it might give way to his needs somehow.

"Don't stop, Junior. Keep a comin'. That's it. See, there you go. The answer to your prayers."

There it was. Old Timer was standing next to a huge fallen sycamore tree whose branches and large trunk, in their stormy search for the ground, had smashed a large section of fence. Junior stepped over a broken board and followed his friend down the bank to the river.

"Don't think about it, Junior. Just jump in and start swimmin'. Follow me to the other side."

Junior stepped, then fell, into the water, which seemed cooler than he expected this time of year. The young colt had worked up a sweat during the events of the evening and was breathing quite hard from the run. He thought he'd be able to walk several yards out into the stream but the bank dropped off quickly. He was already swimming with his head barely above water. Where was Old Timer? As he swam out toward the middle of the river, the current became stronger and he realized he was being swept downstream very quickly. He thought he saw Old Timer out in front of him but it was hard to tell. The moon was going down behind the trees that lined the riverbank and it was hard to distinguish his friend's black figure in the darkness of the night.

He began to tire. After all, this had been quite a night. He had not been eating or sleeping very well lately, still recuperating from the awful acid treatment. The extraordinary weight he carried on his front feet became more and more apparent as the young horse struggled to stay afloat. Junior thought he must be close to the middle of the waterway when he began to realize he might not make it to the other side. The rain that had begun to fall suddenly became heavier, and Junior was still not sure where Old Timer was. He thought he saw him and swam toward the dark figure he thought was Old Timer. It didn't seem to be moving. The current took him toward it then away from it again. With extra effort he swam toward the object. He felt something underneath his feet and realized that the dark figure was a small bush growing in the middle of a sandbar or small island in the middle of the river, and not his missing friend. The exhausted colt climbed up on the little island to rest and check his bearings. He'd done enough swimming for now.

Where was Old Timer? Junior was beginning to feel deserted and insecure again. The rain was falling so hard it was difficult to see much at all. What should he do? He was tired. It was nice to be on dry land again, even if the land was a puny clump of sand not much bigger than he was. He turned his back to the wind, hung his head, and closed his eyes to rest for a while.

When he awoke, the water was above his ankles though the rain had ceased. It had rained enough to bury his little island sanctuary and to make the river seem angrier, swifter.

"Did you have a nice rest, Junior?" Old Timer was standing beside him.

"Where have you been? You left me. You are supposed to be my guide."

"I was always with you, Junior. Don't ever doubt that. I knew you needed rest, so I let you rest. Now, it's time for action. You must trust me."

"Trust you? You deserted me. I almost drowned."

"No, Junior, I would never desert you. You know that. I am here to help you. Now, pull yourself together. You've got some more swimmin' to do."

"Oh, I don't know, I ..."

"Well, you can't stay here forever can you? You don't want to go back to Sammy Lee's barn, do you?"

"No, I guess not."

"All right, then. Let's get goin'. The current has picked up some and it will take you downstream. Keep swimmin' for the bank, okay? It's right over there. Don't stop swimmin' until you reach the other side. You got it?"

"Okay, Socks. You look more like Socks, now, than Old Timer. Why is that?"

"Don't be worryin' about how I look, Junior. The only thing you need to have on your mind right now is swimmin' across this river. Now, come on!"

He could have sworn he felt his friend nudge him out into the fast moving stream. Whether he did or not, Junior was now swimming as hard as he could for the opposite bank. Socks was right, the current had definitely picked up and as hard as he was swimming, it seemed like he was moving quickly down stream while making little progress toward the shore.

Though the rain had stopped, it was all he could do to keep his head above water, his eyes on his goal. He knew where he had to go and he was determined to get there. A strong sense of survival had come over the young colt. He realized it really was a life or death struggle he was immersed in. He had lost sight of his friend once again, but somehow felt he was near. Deep down, he knew that Socks would not abandon him without reason.

As he got nearer to the riverbank, he realized that it was covered with vegetation. Trees with low-lying limbs and branches hanging out over the water were surrounded by all kinds of brush. It was a solid mass. How would he ever get ashore? There was no place to get a foothold, to climb up. There was no beach. He could hear Sock's voice in his ear saying, "No matter what, don't stop swimming." How would he get ashore? Off to his left he thought he saw an opening in the brush. It was down stream, but if he kept swimming as he was, maybe the current would take him to it. If he missed it, he would be out of luck. There might not be another clearing for miles. He swam hard for the bank, keeping an eye on the opening in the vegetation.

The bank was just within reach when he felt something jab him in the side. It was another fallen tree. This one had fallen in the water. Junior could feel the branches against his legs and, all of a sudden, he stopped moving. The river's current swept past him. He was going nowhere. He tried swimming harder, but still didn't move. One of the larger branches had slipped up between his blanket and his tail set. He was caught. The tree had a hold of the leather harness of his tail set and it was not about to let go. All of Junior's efforts at forward progress were thwarted by one branch of this fallen tree. He began to panic. Now, what? Did Old Timer-Socks have a solution for this? Where was he, by the way?

"I'm right here, Junior, up on the bank."

"I'm caught, Old Timer. I didn't see these branches. I was headed for the clearing. Now, I'm stuck, really stuck!" The whole time he was talking, Junior was thrashing around, trying to break free. He knew he couldn't tread water forever. "What do I do, Old Timer, can't you help me? You said you were my guide, my guide to the other side."

"That's right, Junior. I said that and I meant it. Just hang in there, Son. Tread water, and try to conserve your energy while I think."

"You better think of something pretty quick 'cause I feel like I'm sinking!"

Junior was stirring up the water around him by thrashing about so much. He swallowed quite a bit of it. He got some up his nose. He began coughing and spitting.

"Junior, Junior, you need to calm down."

"How can I calm down? I'm going to drowned here in a few minutes."

"What you need to do is reach to your right with your front legs. Paddle to the right, up stream. Try to feel what's underneath you. See how this tree has fallen down at an angle from the bank? The trunk is on your right. See if you can touch it with your feet."

The frantic colt did as his friend suggested. "All I feel down there is a bunch of branches scratching and poking... Wait! I feel it! I can feel the trunk, now. I'm standing on the trunk, sort of. It's slippery."

"Okay, great. Now, I want you to climb up the trunk toward the shore."

"Say what?"

"Climb up the trunk, toward the shore. It's got lots of branches coming out of it, right, like the one you're hung up on?"

"Yeah, I suppose it does."

"Well, use it like a ladder Junior. Get a foothold wherever you can and work yourself up this way. I'm standin' here on dry land, not twenty feet from you, where the roots of this mighty tree pulled out of the ground. Now, come on. You can do it. I know you can."

"But, what about the branch that's caught in my tail set harness?"

"Don't worry about that; just start climbin', crawlin', and scratchin' your way up here 'fore I come down there and pull you up by your ears."

Junior began to see the wisdom in his old friend's advice. The tree trunk felt pretty solid, not as solid as good ol' mother earth, but solid enough to get a hold of. And, it led to the right place. He could see that now. He wasn't sure how he was doing it, but out of sheer will power, if nothing else, he began to scramble his way toward the bank. His feet kept slipping off the trunk and were on either side of it. The colt was actually using it as Old Timer had said, as a sort of ladder up to the bank. Almost immediately he felt resistance. He still had that big branch caught in his harness.

"Pull, Junior. Pull with your front legs. Pull hard with both of them at once. Come on! Wrap those front legs around somethin' solid and pull yourself up."

Junior did as Old Timer said. He pulled as hard as he could until the branch snapped. He was free, free from that at least. When it snapped, he fell forward and kept climbing and crawling with his front legs, and kicking with his back. When he felt solid ground underneath his feet, and saw Socks standing there, part of him wanted to collapse on the spot. The other part wanted to get as far away from that nasty ol' river as he could. He struggled through the thistles, briars, and wild blackberries to follow his mentor and guide to safety.

They soon walked out into the clearing that Junior had spotted from the water. It was larger than he imagined. There was a wooden boat dock at the water's edge, and from the river the meadow fanned out to include some horse paddocks, two barns, and a large house. Junior could see that there were lights on in the house as he suddenly realized how totally exhausted he was. His blanket was torn in several places, his tail set hanging to one side. He had numerous cuts and scratches, some from the submerged tree and some from the thistles and thorns he had to plow through to reach this clearing.

"Well, Junior, you made it. You're gonna be all right, now. You're finally free of Sammy Lee Belford and his cronies."

"Oh, Old Timer, I sure would like to believe that. Won't they come after us?"

"Let's just wait and see what happens."

Junior was eyeing his old friend, who was no longer old, with wonder. Old Timer was a healthy young horse like the one he had seen in his dream. He had no cuts or scratches from crashing through the woods. He wasn't even wet! And what about the gate? Old Timer had smashed – running full speed – right into that wooden gate back at the Belford place. He wasn't even injured? Junior had seen him go down.

"What's going on here, Old Timer?"

"What do you mean?"

"I mean, why do you look like this? You're young again. You're not hurt. You don't have a scratch on you. What's going on?"

"I've crossed over, Junior. I've crossed that River."

"I know you crossed the river; so did I."

"No, you don't understand, Son. I have crossed The River. I died back there at the gate."

Junior felt a chill. "But you're here. You've been with me all the way."

"I will always be here when you need me, Junior. Now, I've got one more thing to do, then I'm off to join ol' Chief, and Traveler, and the rest of those who have gone before. I want you to follow me just a little farther up the hill, if you can."

"I sure would like to rest, Old Timer, Socks."

"I know, I know. Just a little bit farther then you can rest."

Junior was beginning to understand the enormity of what his old friend had just told him. "You died for me, Old Timer? You crashed into that gate so I could escape? And it killed you?" he asked as they walked up the hill.

"It was my time, Junior. I was old. I might have had a heart attack just from that run and all the excitement – the fire and all that."

"Yeah, but you didn't. You smashed the gate so I could get out."

"Junior, life is a temporary assignment – really, just a short work-out in the overall scheme of things. I've lived a very long time compared to most. I'm glad I could do somethin' useful – help a friend – on my way out. I'm no special hero or nothin', Junior. So don't you go on and on about it. I just did what was right. After all, isn't it better to try to do what's right, even if it means you might get hurt, than to play it safe and stand there and watch the world go by?

"Remember what Chief told you in a dream once, Son? He said, 'Be bold, and mighty forces will come to your aid.' Well that was meant for me, I think, as well as you. It took a lot of courage for you to run from Sammy and them, to run out of a burnin' barn, and keep runnin'. Most horses run back to what they think is the safety of their stall in a fire and it ends up killin' 'em."

"But I had Traveler, and Chief, and the other spirit horses to help me."

"Exactly. 'Be bold, and mighty forces...'"

"Well, what do we do, now? I sure would like to lay down and rest."

"You can lay down now if you like. We're close enough."

"Close enough to what?"

"Just you lay down and rest. You've come a long way, Junior, a long way. I've got to go now. But don't you worry. I'm goin' to a much better place. A place where there are no Sammy Lee Belford's, or Ellis Walsh's, or Leonard Rust's, or Paul Chambers', no Walking Horse industry built on the backs of innocent, tortured animals.

"If you ever need anythin', ever want to talk to your old friend, all you have to do is think of me and I'll be there. Happy trails, Junior, until we meet again."

SIXTEEN

Junior lay down to rest on the grass in front of the big house as the young Old Timer walked away into the darkness. Was that a Dalmatian pup running along side his old friend? It sure looked like it.

In the house, the old man said goodnight to his son and his family and went up to bed. Hours later he still could not sleep, unable to get the events of the day out of his mind. He had gone to see an old friend, ran into an old enemy, and wound up stirring up emotions that could find no solace. His heart ached for the young horse in the stall next to Socks. It ached for the thousands of horses just like him who were going through the same kind of torment.

Royal Riggins got out of bed, slipped on some clothes and boots and walked outside into the warm August night. The air was clean and fresh after the rain. Water still dripped from the leaves. The crickets and frogs were in full voice. He had just sat down in one of the rocking chairs on the back porch when he noticed something, or someone, coming toward him across the lawn. He stood up and rubbed his face in disbelief as he peered out through the mist at the approaching apparition. What he saw – or thought he saw – took him back about thirty years or so to a time when his old Dalmatian, Midnight, used to like to hang around a certain black gelding he had in training.

As Roy walked down the steps to get a better look, the pair turned away to their right and down the hill toward the woods and the river. When they turned they both caught his eye and seemed to beckon him to follow. After a moment's hesitation he ambled down the hill after them. He was doing a pretty good running walk for an eighty-something year-old horse trainer when he realized that Socks and Midnight had vanished into the night. They were nowhere to be seen. He was sure he wasn't sleepwalking. What had he really seen? And what was this?

Junior heard the man coming down the hill and struggled to his feet. Not sure exactly what he should do, he stood his ground and waited for the man to get closer.

"It's all right, boy. I'm not going to hurt you. Easy, now." Junior recognized the voice of the man who had visited Old Timer earlier that day. Was that really just a few hours ago? It seemed like a lifetime. He was sure it was the same man.

"Whoa, now. It's all right. Just let me get a hold of your halter. That's it. Where did you come from? You shouldn't be running around here loose like this. Come on, now. Let's get a better look at you."

Royal Riggins led Junior up to the barn, turned the inside lights on, and put him in the crossties. The other horses called out to them, curious about the late night intrusion. He removed the colt's misaligned tail set and torn blanket. There were remnants of leg wraps still clinging to the horse's legs, which he also removed. He filled a bucket with warm water and gave Junior a good sponge bath, being extra gentle around the numerous cuts and scrapes. After toweling the colt dry, he found some appropriate medication for the cuts in a cabinet in the tack room. Ricky Riggins, seeing the lights on in the barn, came to investigate.

"I thought I heard you get up, Dad. What are you doing down here at this ... who's this?"

"I don't know, Son. No, wait! I think I do know this colt. He's the colt that was in the stall next to Socks over at Belford's barn."

"Can't be."

"I know it sounds impossible, but look at him. He came from somewhere. Look at the way his blanket is torn up, and his tail set half off, all these cuts. He was soaking wet, too. As strange as it sounds, I think he escaped somehow then swam across the river, and scrambled through the woods to end up here. That would explain it, wouldn't it?"

"Maybe, except it seems highly unlikely that he could do all that on his own."

"Do you have another explanation?"

"Well, no. If you're sure it's him."

"The more I look at him, I'm sure. He looks a lot like ol' Chief, doesn't he? Besides, maybe he wasn't alone. Maybe he had help."

"What do you mean? You think someone let him out and brought him all the way over here?"

"Maybe." Roy Riggins was about to tell his son about seeing Socks and Midnight – or thinking he did – but decided to keep it to himself for the time being. The two men put Junior in an empty stall, gave him a flake of hay and made sure he had water, then went back to the house to try to get some sleep.

The local morning news had a live report from "Sammy Belford Stables, a highly successful Tennessee Walking Horse training facility. One person, and at least twelve expensive show horses, is believed dead in what authorities are already calling a suspicious overnight fire. The blaze, as you can see, has almost completely consumed this magnificent show barn, home to some of the area's top show horses. Fire officials are still investigating, of course, but I'm told that preliminary reports indicate the fire may have started in the storeroom, the result of an explosion of hazardous chemicals kept on the premises. What exactly these chemicals may have been used for has yet to be determined. Witnesses said they heard several loud explosions during the course of the fire. We will return to you with more details, as the situation develops. Back to you, Dan."

"Alicia, is there any evidence to indicate these chemicals may have been used for the so-called 'soring' practices that have often been rumored to be used by some Walking Horse trainers?"

"As I said, Dan, it's really too early to tell much at this point, but that is one of the possibilities this reporter will be looking in to."

"Wow, do you think we ought to call them and tell them we have one of their horses, Dad?"

"Let's give it some time, Son, and see what happens. I can tell you one thing, that colt is in no hurry to be back in the hands of Sammy Lee Belford. Besides, they've probably already got him down on their list of fatalities for the insurance company."

Father and son looked at each other knowingly and simultaneously said, "Are you thinking what I'm thinking?"

EPILOGUE

Royal and Ricky Riggins removed Junior's shoes later that day and discovered the springs and ball bearings. They were able to purchase the young bay stallion from Mrs. Armistead for a modest sum under the implied condition that they would keep quiet about what they knew. Of course, Royal Riggins never made any explicit promise to bury the truth. He and Ricky both knew they would have plenty to say when the time was right.

Junior found peace in his new home and people who take good care of him. He misses Old Timer but still talks to his old friend when the spirit moves him and knows that he, too, has gone home.

Sammy Lee, in turn, had a ready explanation for the presence of so many toxic and hazardous chemicals in his storeroom, which contributed so readily to the fire. However, thanks to the persistence of a certain investigative reporter, local news media began extensive coverage of the illegal and unethical practices that run rampant through the entire industry that calls itself the Pride of Tennessee.

GLOSSARY

Canter: A three-beat collected gallop.

Collected: A horse is collected when he is flexing to the bit and working off his hind legs and light on his front.

Collodion: Also called proxlyin solution and nitrocotton solution. Made from proxylin, ethanol, and diethyl ether. Is a pale yellow, syrupy liquid that acts as a sealant and can cause damage to the central nervous system.

Coronet Band: The lowest part of the pastern of a horse, just above the hoof.

Crossties: A pair of chain or rope restraints snapped to a horse's halter (one on each side) to hold him in place while grooming.

Crotonal: Crotonaldehyde is a liquid that is corrosive and toxic. Contact with skin causes severe irritation and possible second degree burns. Is so strong it is cut with kerosene before applied to horse's legs.

Crupper: That part of a harness that fits under the tail.

Curb Chain: A small chain attached to the bit that fits underneath a horse's chin. When the shank of the bit is pulled back the chain tightens against the chin.

DMSO: Dimethyl sulfoxide is a byproduct of the wood industry, a commercial solvent. Is used as a carrier to help soring chemicals such as diesel fuel, kerosene, and Gibson's liniment penetrate the skin.

Flat Walk: The slower four-beat gait of the Tennessee Walking Horse.

Gelded: Castrated

Get: Offspring

Hock: The joint in the hind leg of the horse corresponding to the ankle in man, but raised from the ground and thus appearing as if bent backward.

Mustard Oil: Allyl isothiocyanate is highly toxic and a known carcinogen and mutagenic. Causes severe burns, blisters and scars.

Near Side: The side of a horse one usually mounts from. The horse's left side.

Off Side: The side opposite the near side. The horse's right side.

Pastern: The part of a horse's foot between the fetlock and the hoof.

Running Walk: The faster four-beat gait of the Tennessee Walking Horse.

Salicylic acid: 2-hydroxy-benzoic acid is used to remove or reduce scars from show horse's legs by causing a sloughing off of the skin. The pain of this procedure is so intense it is said to have caused death in some cases. Horses remain sore for an additional week or so after the initial three-day ordeal.

Trotting Balls: Also known as rattlers or rollers. Training "action" devices used on some gaited horses consisting of metal, wooden, or plastic hollowed spheres aligned on a leather strap much like beads on a necklace.

Twitch: A restraining device applied to an animal's nose. Can be made of rope and then twisted, or of metal and tightened as a vice. Effectively pinches the nose to divert attention from other unpleasantness.

AUTHOR'S NOTE

Though this is a novel in which horses talk to each other and have vision and insight beyond their supposed capabilities, do not discount the amount of truth contained in these pages. All non-historical characters in this story, both human and equine, are fictional, however, many have been drawn from composites or variations of real life characters known to the author. The depictions of training practices and soring methods used in this book have all been either witnessed first hand by the author or accounted to him by undeniably reliable sources. If you doubt their authenticity, please investigate the matter yourself. If you don't doubt it, please do whatever you can to put an end to this horrible tragedy.

Concerned Readers may wish to contact one or more of the following organizations:

ASPCA
www.aspca.org

Sound Horse Organization
www.walkinghorse.org

Steppin Out
www.walkinghorsenews.com

The Gaited Horse
www.thegaitedhorse.com

HSUS
www.hsus.org

USDA
www.aphis.usda.gov

U.S. House of Representatives
www.house.gov

U.S. Senate
www.senate.gov

BIBLIOGRAPHY

AND SUGGESTED READING

Biography Of The Tennessee Walking Horse
By Ben A. Green
Copyright, 1960